A QUESTION OF HOLLOWNESS

by

JAMES I. MCGOVERN

WingSpan Press

Published in the United States and the United Kingdom by WingSpan Press, Livermore, CA

The WingSpan name, logo and colophon are the trademarks of WingSpan Publishing.

ISBN 978-1-63683-075-9 (pbk.)
ISBN 978-1-63683-937-0 (ebk.)

First edition 2025

Printed in the United States of America

www.wingspanpress.com

Also by James I. McGovern

Fiction

The Child Abuse Man
Aura of Purgatory
The Twin Fortunes and Other Stories
Beyond the Failure Club
A Truly Higher Life Form
Account of a Minor Haunting
The Wine Cork Collector
The Young Widow's Trauma
Stories of Disillusionment

Non-Fiction

Religion as Reinforcement in Hemingway

Verse

The Celtic Laborer

CONTENTS

A QUESTION OF HOLLOWNESS

1.

This is the story of Dysmas, my childhood friend who now rests beneath a stone inscribed with just his given name and year of death. That's in rural California, but he grew up in the Midwest. There were eight children born into the family but the eldest—a boy—died of pneumonia early on. Dysmas was third-born and had one other brother, younger than him, but the child fell out of a tree when he was about to start school. My friend was thus left with five sisters, one older and four younger, the eldest honored with one of the two actual bedrooms in their house. Dysmas slept in the attic space with the younger ones but had to be moved out as they successively reached puberty. He replaced his older sister in her exclusive bedroom, she being moved upstairs to the female quarters. The young woman greatly resented this and harbored an intense dislike for her brother.

Our town was a nondescript suburb easily impacted by economic downturns. Dysmas with his family of ten felt the effects far more than I with my family of four. We were nonetheless friends due to our being classmates and living close to each other. The village, as it was called, and our school provided nothing in the way of youth activities, so we were often idle in each other's company. There were woods and ragged fields nearby where we would prowl, and creek beds where we'd hide. Dysmas would want to wrestle sometimes in the grass and dust, and he'd get very aggressive, as if he were angry. It always ended with my having him in a hold he couldn't escape but his refusing to "give," so I'd concede him the win out of boredom. We got dirty enough at these times such that I was told to bathe before dinner, though I never heard of Dysmas having to.

Corporal punishment, even to a severe degree, was acceptable at the time, and my friend's father freely indulged in it. Multiple hard slaps could be expected for even the least significant infraction, and at any place or time. On one occasion while driving, the father swung

3

his arm across Dysmas to strike his eldest sister in the right passenger seat. On another night Dysmas was awakened by his father slapping the young woman around the living room. Having come in late, she escaped to the attic stairs past her alarmed brother. He continued on and saw his father sulking.

"What's going on?" the son asked.

"Nothing," came the hoarse reply. "Go back to bed."

He obeyed, sensing his sister's pain and humiliation above, his mother no doubt hiding in the parental bedroom. But she wasn't above such practice herself, utilizing a paddle with more controlled blows. Yet she also was a victim, Dysmas knew, judging from some telltale noise behind their door. For many years a crib had been in there, each of its occupants witnessing the procreation of the next.

The father had been greatly affected by the loss of his youngest son, whom he'd cherished as a "real boy," epitomizing the rough-and-ready nature the father believed was his own. At the dinner table and other times, Dysmas would often catch a gratuitous scowl directed at him, as if his father were thinking: "So this is what I'm left with, this sissy and a gaggle of girls." The look was devastating and Dysmas cowered before it.

The question of identity came to light as we entered adolescence. When my friend was out sick from school a few days, I was joined on the long walk home by a girl from our class. Dysmas, upon his return, was startled to see her continue to appear at my side for the walk. We started out from school as a trio, me in the middle and the girl in high spirits, but it didn't last for long.

"Why do you want to walk with us?" Dysmas demanded.

"Why do I—want—well, I guess just to be friendly. That's okay, isn't it?"

"But you weren't that friendly before, so why now?"

The girl turned into our local dime store as we passed it, muttering a faint farewell to me.

"What's your problem?" I inquired of Dysmas.

"I just get sick of them," came his answer.

Shortly thereafter he informed our teacher, a nun, that he wished to become a priest. Our pastor had arranged a tour of seminary school and the seminary itself for up to five boys from our class. Dysmas was put on the list and the nun included me to round out the carful. On the appointed day, my friend was in the front seat between the priest, who was driving, and a boy who'd already committed to the priesthood. I rode in the back with two other low prospects. I watched Dysmas in his absorption with priestly talk, ignoring the banter of my seatmates. A flicker of envy passed through me that I quickly dismissed. The tours of the institutes went pretty well, but we remained in conversational groups—three of us discussing the religious life, two talking of sports and girls, and myself with a sense of separation growing between me and my friend.

His plans hit a wall when he broached them to his parents. His mother saw him reading the brochures that that arrived from the diocesan institutes and other religious orders. Her reaction was thinly veiled fear as she warned him of the hazards of missionary work and permanent isolation from family and friends. His father was quickly informed, no doubt stifling his initial reaction since well aware of the penalty for blocking a vocation: going straight to hell upon dying. Instead he took an indirect approach, suggesting at dinner that traveling to and from the seminary school would be very difficult. Dysmas would have to reside at his grandmother's house in the city with his bachelor uncles and spinster aunt. He'd sleep in the low-ceilinged attic and ride a smelly city bus twice a day with low-lifers and bums. Dysmas was told he should think very carefully about these changes.

My friend didn't give up. He went to the rectory to see the pastor, hoping to gain his intervention, but was met by his assistant, a young priest who was the school's ersatz youth counselor. The assistant was saddled with various non-priestly duties such as lawn mowing and driving the school's bus, so he listened to Dysmas with a drowsy countenance. His posture appeared the same as that he had in the confessional while listening to someone's sins. He promised, however, that they'd talk with my friend's father, ending the session on an appropriate upbeat note.

The father grew more taciturn in the following days, then revealed at supper that he'd talked with one of the priests.

"They'll be putting you in the parish quota for St. Mike's," he said to Dysmas.

It was a standard high school for boys with three levels of study: college prep, business, and shop. One's classes for all four years were determined by a placement test taken during eighth grade. My friend was stunned.

"What happened with seminary school?"

"Ah, well. You'll be in a Catholic school, a good atmosphere to think that over longer."

As if he were making a concession, Dysmas thought, in accepting the expense over the free public school. But he'd wanted the eldest sister to attend the girls' school, continue with the nuns to guard her virginity, and she'd rejected him. The unused funds for that simply enabled the father's budgeting.

"But I've thought it all through already," Dysmas protested.

"It's done," said his father, vigorously cutting some meat.

Nothing more was said about it until Dysmas had left the table. He listened from his room to his mother's murmurs of support for her husband, the man more assertive but also speaking low. Only emphatic fragments could be understood.

"It's a wasted life," his father said.

Then, later: "They're all parasites."

———◆———

Despite his lackadaisical attitude toward the placement test, Dysmas landed on the high college prep track at St. Michael's. I was assigned to the business curriculum, far less demanding but still meeting entrance requirements at many colleges. Our time together was much reduced by my friend's course work, leading me to socialize with a girl with whom we'd graduated. This irritated Dysmas, predictably I considered, and it wasn't long before Margaret caught on.

"What's wrong with him?" she asked.

"I'm not sure."

"Doesn't he know you can have more than one friend?"

"He must. He's supposed to be smarter than me."

Dysmas went out for wrestling hoping to vent his frustrations. He quickly found, however, that it was much different than our rolling in the dust. You could be counted out. You could lose on points. You couldn't win by boring your opponent into quitting. You couldn't enjoy his hold as you lay there with him.

"Think he might like my friend Lynn?" Margaret asked.

I thought for a moment, pictured Dysmas and my gripping his head in the dust, hearing his low laugh.

"No, I don't think so. Not just now."

"When, then?"

"I don't know. Maybe never,"

"You should tell him to grow up."

"He might be worse then."

Dysmas had to struggle with his school courses, often working deep into the evening to finish for the next day. The noises of the household pushed his efforts to the basement. When we both went out for track, he had to quit when his grades plummeted. It was just as well. The coach had removed him from our middle-distance group and made him a backup hurdler, which meant he handled the hurdles for the older boys. During summer my friend had little respite. His mother now required his assistance with the younger girls, the eldest off working as a waitress, and he also did the family's laundry. When I'd see him he always looked morose, said little, showed no interest in the future or events of the day.

My friend seemed to find his niche on our return to St. Mike's, joining the speech club and showing unusual vigor and determination in debates. He performed impressively in a tournament with an older partner and retained his position on the team. His aggressive manner irritated some, however, and the following year he was demoted to junior varsity. Angered by this, he quit the club and joined me at cross-country practices. The running and physical strain seemed a welcome vent for his frustrations, which had included his being fired from a summer job. That had resulted from his dropping a pile of dishes in front of a testy restaurant manager.

"That was dumb," the angry man had scowled.

"So fire me!" Dysmas responded.

"All right, you're fired!"

It had not set well with his parents and earned him a return to full household duties. All of this seemed expressed in his heavy breaths as he ran beside me at the practices. He was still struggling with his studies, staying up late over them, and was not in condition for the running. He frequently lagged in the longer exercises, especially when we ran for time. I'd fall in then with Peter, a thin soft-spoken youth with effortless graceful strides. We'd exchange ironic, amusing quips as we ran, forgetting we were in a competitive sport. We'd lingered a few times in the showers together, he olive-skinned and I quite fair, each more conscious of the other than the self. The ironic quips continued but the friendship went no further. That was something Dysmas didn't understand—couldn't, because it required a type of control he did not possess.

One day, during a long conditioning run, I found I'd lost track of both Dysmas and Peter. They were still missing as all the runners finished and gathered around our coach, some freshman stragglers the last ones in. One of them, a small peppery lad, approached the coach and announced that Dysmas had beat up Peter.

"Where are they now?" asked the coach, who was one of the religious brothers.

"In the bushes around the backstretch."

The brother looked up in the indicated direction, then turned to one side as he noticed Peter approaching, not running but almost staggering, one hand to his head.

"Find Dysmas and take him to the athletic office," the coach told the student manager. "Have him turn in his sweats."

The manager set out with two of the senior runners.

<hr />

While the mother of Dysmas was shocked by his expulsion from St. Michael's, his father took it in stride. He chose to see the reason as fighting, period. He needed no backstory since now he could see his son as better than a sissy. In addition, he was freed from the exorbitant tuition charges and even had a refund coming. Dysmas could finish up at the public school with no blame due his parents since they'd done their best to obey Church dictates. The parasitic religious had simply sabotaged their efforts.

Dysmas himself was sullen and closemouthed about the affair, even with me, showing no further interest in Peter or his recovery. The courses at the public high school involved little homework or study, so Dysmas had much more free time. Not wishing to spend it at home, he joined the drama club as a stagehand, refusing a couple of bit parts he was offered. He also assisted in the library for minimal pay. He was seen to keep mostly to himself, but he faked some interest in a shy, plain-looking girl to cover issues about sexual preference. He took up smoking, his persona becoming a match for the loafers around the school.

Yet he told me he planned to attend Notre Dame University.

"How are you going to swing *that*?" I asked him.

"I'm good at taking tests, so I can handle the entrance exams, and my grade average is up from the snap courses I've been taking. And I've had plenty of school activities, on paper anyway."

"What about the tuition? Sky-high."

"It'll be covered by the U.S. Navy, after I get a regular—not walk-on—appointment to their ROTC unit there."

"How will you get them to appoint you?"

"I'll handle their tests like I will with N.D. Except some are physical. But I'll knock off smoking and work out for a while. Play up my activities like with N.D."

"You really think this will work for you?"

"Sure! Why wouldn't it?"

"It must be very competitive."

"Yeah. So beat the competition."

"Well, good luck to you."

9

I didn't want to discourage him. He was clearly in comeback mode and still my friend. While the priestly ambition had dissipated, he was still purposeful and intense to a religious degree, so I could only accommodate him. So it appeared to me, anyway.

Dysmas was admitted to Notre Dame and somehow gained the only NROTC scholarship for his graduating class. There were three such appointments for our class at St. Michael's, where Dysmas certainly would not have qualified. This was of great satisfaction to him, vindicating his past actions and transfer. His smugness was short-lived, however. All three of the St. Michael scholars received appointments to their first choices, one of them to Notre Dame, but Dysmas did not. He was informed that, since the unit at N.D. was full, he was appointed to his carelessly designated second choice, the main campus of our state university. Dysmas spent some weeks mulling the greatly reduced benefits of this prospect, then declined the scholarship. He lost interest in serious college planning but, since the Vietnam war was looming, enrolled at a local junior college to protect his student draft deferment.

———•———

Having decided that junior college was too much like high school, Dysmas joined me a year later at a branch of the state university. We commuted into the nearby city, where I studied business and he was in the college of liberal arts with no declared major. This became his prolonged status as he only took courses which pleased him. He was a dilettante, I decided, though he was very good at some things. These were chiefly recreational, like chess and handball, so I thought he might be on a long vacation from the strictures of his first high school and home life. When I suggested he try something that could give his life direction, he tried to start a new student activity, Softball Players Against the War, which the dean of students summarily rejected.

"That might not have been realistic," I told Dysmas. "It kind of put him on the spot professionally."

10

"Realistic," my friend repeated, reflecting through cigarette smoke. "That's a slippery concept now."

He'd grown his hair long and added a beard. He'd have fit in well at the abundant protests but chose the loner route instead. He did not misuse drugs as far as I knew.

"How do you mean?" I asked.

"There's the factories," he said after a pause.

"What about them?"

"The people in them are in a different world from us, our sitting around in a student lounge, sipping coffee. Though they have coffee too, of course. But in a different reality."

Dysmas was working during every break from school, and sometimes evenings after classes. The jobs had been in factories, mail facilities, a youth camp, but he avoided restaurants after the broken dishes incident. He was also wary of department stores after failing a lie detector test about stealing. His earnings went mostly for a cheap apartment he rented after leaving his family.

"So then," I said to him, "a different world. A different reality. But there are many different realities. The people in glass office buildings, the people on farms, et cetera. Different worlds, in a sense. But there are commonalities that run between them. Very similar standards, concepts, interests. We haven't much choice but to recognize them, live by them, to be truly realistic, succeed with other people."

Dysmas looked at me blankly, then looked away.

"Other people," he said. "Realistic. Succeed. Many brands of bull out there."

I waited him out as he took in smoke.

"Thing is," he continued, "you've got this whole world of people running around in circles for the short span of their lives. Trying to achieve, competing, killing each other. And in the end what do any of them have? An obit they can't even read. A stone or something on the dirt above their heads. Or maybe just get blasted to bits in some war. They never end, you know. The complete asses are the critical masses. Always."

This is my friend, I told myself. What is happening to him? And I thought of a girl he'd hung out with recently, an owl-eyed waif from his literature class.

"Do you still see Sally these days?"

He exhaled with exasperation.

"She wanted me to come out to Tower Lake at Christmas, meet her relatives and stuff. I had that seasonal job at the postal facility, miss one day and you're fired. So I didn't go. Also never got back to her on it. Just didn't show up and never called her about it. She'd called my parents' house trying to reach me, but I didn't call back. After the term started I saw her here with some other girls. Our eyes locked but I just kept walking. Nothing was said. Nothing connects us now. There's just an abyss, a rift."

I waited for him to continue, but he was sulking. I sensed he was fighting regrets.

"Well," I responded, "you had your priority. A necessary one. No one should blame you for what you did."

I wouldn't mention the way he did it.

"It was rotten," Dysmas said. "I was tired of her and needed the money but yeah, it was rotten. Excuses are useless. Each and every act of ours is a decision on some level. We are all responsible for all our actions or inactions, all our decisions."

This would be our last true conversation for some time. Dysmas soon after crashed his old car into a brick wall while high on marijuana. He was not seriously injured but two days later dropped out of school and enlisted in the Air Force. Though an airman first class, he could not fly due to insufficient eyesight, so he was sent to language school in Virginia to learn Laotian, supposedly in preparation for some exotic appointment. He wound up, however, at an isolated facility in the Texas dust bowl, working as a file clerk with little to no diversion. He became noticeably depressed and was discharged from the Air Force as a mild schizoid, having served for well under a year.

Rather than return to the Midwest, Dysmas drifted to San Francisco, where he took a room in the apartment of a Chinese family over a store they operated. It was not their primary residence, and his room was at first filled with junk which he moved to a cluttered backyard. He was permitted to share meals with the family, which they prepared from stock in their store and seafood they caught themselves. The other steady residents in the apartment were two young women who shared a room much nicer than Dysmas's. He came to realize they were not related to the family and, while one was of Chinese heritage, the other was Laotian. They'd apparently been caught up in the general chaos of southeast Asia and somehow found their way across the sea. Dysmas tried a little of his Air Force Laotian with the one woman, but she simply laughed at his efforts.

As his military pay ran out, Dysmas worked in shipping and receiving for a company near the waterfront. It was strenuous toil, exhausting for a recent file clerk. He could hardly stay awake during supper before landing unconscious on his rollaway bed. He adjusted rather quickly, however, accepting the strain and pain as a sort of penance for ambiguous sins. He even took to strolling the nearby neighborhoods, wandering among the hippies and lowlifes of the time, finding drugs and desperation as the surrogates for peace and love. There was one smoky den that felt in tune with his feelings, so he entered. Amber light struggled through the haze, the clientele mostly male, and there would've been only low mutterings if it weren't for an insane poet shouting his creations near the back. Dysmas stared at him hatefully, then felt a tug on his sleeve.

"Know what you're thinking," the man beside him chuckled. "Looking for this, maybe? Tijuana gold."

He was shorter than Dysmas, hirsute with floppy hat, and held out a couple of packets.

"How much?"

They negotiated a price, Dysmas supposedly getting three for the price of two.

"I'm here every night," the man informed him.

But Dysmas didn't make the place his exclusive haunt, visiting other dives as well and mixing with knots of hippies on the streets. They were typically ragged and trite in their conversation, their free love no doubt sordid. The women, actually just girls, would cadge him for a joint, the young men holding back in a show of self-sufficiency. Dysmas felt flickers of pity for the women, but it quickly turned to disgust. They had *chosen* to get themselves here, to throw themselves at bums.

He began to stay in some nights after supper, reading the street publications or well-thumbed paperbacks. One or the other of his female neighbors would sometimes look in and tease him. He'd reply in kind and return to his reading. There came a night, however, when he'd already slid into sleep but was wakened to find the young Laotian woman, Mali, in bed with him.

His thoughts, his nascent dreams, were drained from his mind. He was unable to move as if made of cement.

"What are you doing here?"

She snuggled against his side as if in answer.

"Ying will see you're gone, maybe rouse Madame."

"No. Ying gets very tired from the work."

They labored as cleaners at a downtown hotel.

"I'm surprised at you, Mali. I don't know what to say."

"Say nothing. Just hold me."

He hesitated. Then, for lack of another response, he extended his arm around her head and touched her shoulder on the far side. Minimal acquiescence. They remained this way a few moments, Dysmas perplexed and vaguely fearful. He tried to think but thought didn't fit the situation. Mali turned into him suddenly and peppered his face with kisses.

Dysmas was holding her upper arms, torn between pushing her away or—against his nature—releasing her, yielding to mutual embrace. He knew what he desperately wanted to do, but this was a girl who'd evaded the power of three or four governments to be here in this bed with him. She was owed something, owed much, and he was the default redeemer. She had the upper ground in this conflict of basic natures.

His resistance melted and a single will ruled the night.

Dysmas awoke in a mist of shame, the gray light of dawn unwelcome in his haven. The disgrace he sensed was massive, incomprehensible, only isolated details available for his analysis. It had not been a dream, he knew, for though Mali was gone an aura of her presence hung about the rollaway. Her fragrance, the ghostly echo of her words, the pain and pleasure of her movements, her energy. Dysmas lay still, assured himself the door was fully closed, let pieces of the world fall into place. His scattered thoughts began to coalesce, then harden into a sure and unequivocal knowledge of guilt. Mortal sin, straight to hell, all of that and yet none of that was the worst of it. He had betrayed his own selfhood, surrendered his nature and knowledge of it in the face of sudden challenge. His was not a noble soul.

"You're just an absurdity," he spoke aloud.

But no, that couldn't be. He wouldn't let it. The sound of his voice reminded him of where and who he was. He had a routine that he'd developed, and he must rise from the bed and follow it. Rise from the dead.

It was not without effort. His motions were stiff and stumbling, a picking through pieces of shattered existence. He bore Mali no ill will. She had simply been following her nature. She had been true, he had not.

He'd have liked to shower in the common bathroom, but he dared not. He had to avoid others' notice of him. He wanted to dress and slip out of the building into the sea of strangers. Get to the loading dock and punish himself by working extra hard. Expiation.

Once he was sure that Mali and Ying had left for work, Dysmas descended and passed through the early bustle of the store. He felt good on the street, just another pedestrian with no apparent connection to catastrophe. But as he wove among the people with their newspapers and morning beverages, the angst of his bedroom and bed itself rose within him ineluctably. He couldn't just follow

15

his routine, he realized, for it would take him back to the place and situation that was his ruin. He sighted a Japanese theater that opened early, craved its darkness, left the familiar route to work for a haven in which to hide and think, sat almost alone before grainy black-and-white scenes of young men climbing Mt. Fuji. He considered what to do about the job, how to quit, and what he would do afterward. He decided he'd better get coffee first, smoke a couple of cigarettes.

When they asked him in personnel where to send his last paycheck, Dysmas gave them my address. It was the only one he recalled aside from his estranged family.

Back at the Chinese store, he told Madame that his mother had died so he must return to the Midwest. She was sympathetic and packed some food for him to eat on the bus. Dysmas stuffed his things into an old duffel bag and soon was on his way.

The bus station was near the hotel where Mali and Ying worked. Dysmas passed it but did not look up at the windows.

2.

Upon his return, Dysmas had dropped by the apartment while Katerina, a classmate from my MBA program, was visiting. It was rather awkward. We'd been casually smoking, discussing our parts of a team project, when the buzzer from the lobby sounded. I answered and buzzed him in, surprised but not very disturbed.

"A childhood friend," I informed Katerina, a svelte and prepossessing young woman.

Dysmas appeared in the foyer, unkempt and travel weary, I guessed. I did introductions.

"Nice to meet you," Kat smiled. She could easily be sophisticated but not condescending.

Dysmas gave a nod and a grunt, his eyes showing surprise, confusion. I invited him in, asked if he'd like a drink.

"Just water," he said.

I got it for him and we sat in a triangle in the parlor of my furnished two-roomer.

"As kids," I said to lighten the mood, "we used to wrestle in the dust. Remember, Dys?"

He gave an embarrassed smile. Kat politely showed interest.

"Better at least than the mud."

I asked about his trip, how he'd been lately, but Dysmas was vague. It was clear he wouldn't talk openly with Kat there. Eventually, despite the smallness of my apartment, I felt I had to ask him if he had a place to stay.

"Yeah, I'm cool on that."

It was the hollow assurance of the street, where I assumed he'd wind up.

"Kat works for the public aid department. She has connections with the shelters. She could maybe—"

"Yes!" she broke in. "I'm sure we could—"

17

But Dysmas was rankled.

"No! I said I'm cool. Really." Then, standing: "I have to go now." I followed him to the door.

"Is there anything you need?" I asked. "Where's your stuff?"

"In the rental outside."

"Oh. Well, don't be a stranger, Dys. Give me a call and we'll shoot some pool or something."

I stood in the hall and watched him turn into the stairway. I half wanted to go down with him, just the two of us talking, but it didn't seem right to leave my classmate. Dysmas and I could talk later.

"Why was he like that?" Katerina asked.

"I'm not sure. It's been building a long time, I think. He wanted to be a priest but his parents wouldn't let him. That's way in the past, though. Must be more to it."

"Yes, there must be."

"Could you use a glass of wine?"

"I could, yes. Just one small glass, though. I want to pass the breathalyzer, if necessary."

After she left I stewed awhile in my armchair. Dysmas had come to me unannounced, in a sorry state, but then who else did he have to go to? Since we were friends, I should be available to him, more so than I had been. But a time might come to set limits. Our lives had moved in different directions, after all, our personalities shaped separately. Yet to some extent I should accommodate him, I decided, follow through on our bonding in the dust.

He was in touch a few days later, apparently wanted to assure me he was all right, getting himself together. He'd landed a taxi job, aided by his veteran status which he'd embellished. The employment got him approved for a basement apartment not far from my own residence. He was game for some friendly competition but demurred on my pool suggestion, opting instead for chess, in which he was more skilled than I and usually won our matches. I readily went along with him, gratified by his upbeat manner. When we met, he filled me in on his experiences in the Air Force and San Francisco. His tone was casual, dismissive, as if those memories were throwaways for a mental trash compactor.

The taxi job was to his liking, free of close supervision and pressure to socialize. He drove by night, cruising the pub and theater district, the blocks of high-end hotels, sometimes taking a fare to the airport and waiting there to take a tired arrival into the city. He enjoyed the night air, the constant movement, the freedom to smoke while working unless a fare objected. He learned from other cabbies how to handle them and which to never pick up. It appeared he was to have an easy slide for a while to balance the knocks and dead ends he had known.

One night in mid-week when business was slow, he was hailed by two men in fancy suits standing in front of an upscale restaurant. When Dysmas pulled over, one man got in but the other held back, hand on the door. The first man was impeccably groomed in addition to expensively dressed, Dysmas sensing a prospective big tip.

"Thanks for stopping," the man smiled.

Dysmas gave a tentative nod. It seemed an odd thing to say. Outside, the second man was gesturing "come on" at the restaurant entrance, from which two more men came trotting out toward the cab. They were dressed more casually than the first two.

"Can't take passengers in front," Dysmas said. "I'd get stopped, lose my license."

"No problem," said the man in back. He turned on the seat and shouted a bit in Spanish at the open door, through which the three men outside piled into the cab.

Dysmas waited, neither approving nor opposing this arrangement, until the first man issued a street address. It was in a restless part of the city, not among the worst but with more than its share of disorder and crime. The men in back talked congenially at first, all in Spanish, then became subdued, silent gaps between serious, low-volume remarks. Dysmas eventually guided the cab into a darkened side street of old bungalows. He was unable to see house numbers so he let the cab creep along slowly, awaiting instructions.

"Stop here," came a coarse voice, not one of the suit wearers.

Dysmas obeyed. Silence followed, the men in back not moving.

"The cash box," said Coarse Voice. "Give!"

Dysmas froze, not comprehending the situation, not wanting to. A heavy metal object slammed into his head near the right temple. He was dazed but suddenly understood, struggled to move toward the glove compartment. He was assisted in this by a vicious shove at the back of his neck. He found the cigar box, typically used at this time when cabbies still gave change for fares.

The men exited when they had the box, laughing once outside, the man who'd first spoken with Dysmas the last to go.

"Don't hang around," he muttered to my friend.

Duly warned, Dysmas put the cab in gear and crept away carefully down the street. He couldn't turn at the first cross street because it was blocked in both directions by people partying or fighting. He kept straight, turning where able to avoid the street activity, eventually reaching a main thoroughfare. There were crowds and ethnic music blaring, but at least he could cruise with the *Not In Service* sign up until he felt faint and pulled to the curb. He managed to get a call off to his night manager before he passed out, briefly awakening to questions from two policemen while he was loaded into an ambulance. He responded to them by again passing out until the following morning when he awoke in a hospital.

Dysmas did not return to the cab company following the robbery. He secluded himself in his basement apartment and allowed few visitors other than me, just one from two younger sisters and one from a fellow driver. He was mostly uncommunicative, somehow blaming himself for his situation, missing a police lineup so that a suspect went free. I let him stew in his feelings, figuring time would heal, brought him groceries and newspapers. After a while he'd go out for walks, starting to notice again the world around him. We played pool once but his game was terrible.

"What will he do now?" Katerina asked me.

"I don't know."

"Does he need a referral? For work or anything?"

"He says he's waiting on something. Someone he met at the cab place gave him a call."

"When was this?"

"A week or two ago, I think. He was vague about it but acted like he didn't need anything else."

"Well, let me know if I can help."

She had very straight flaxen hair that she wore almost shoulder length and never tied back. Her features were strong, her expression knowing. She was willowy and confident. Our relationship had grown beyond the project mates' stage. She became almost as much a part of my life as Dysmas. When I couldn't reach him for a while, either by phone or dropping by his apartment, I wasn't much concerned since Katerina was gaining priority. There lingered a need for contact, however, growing as time passed, so I felt a measure of relief when he finally answered his phone. His tone was surprisingly upbeat as we greeted each other. He explained he'd been working for a vehicle transport service, driving individual cars to distant locations, often bringing one back the other way. It was a great job, he said, mostly on the open road and away from the scumbags he'd had to tolerate before. He suggested we get together for drinks.

"I think we're both tied up for the work week," I said, obliquely referring to Katerina. "How about the weekend?"

"Sure! That'd be great!"

I was quite pleased by this contact, especially by his evident acceptance of Kat. The weekend came and went, however, without his calling or response to my own attempts. On the Tuesday following I accepted a collect long-distance call from a county jail in rural Wisconsin, guessing it was Dysmas. It was. He explained that he'd been stopped for speeding while delivering a Lincoln Continental to Minneapolis. One of the officers thought he smelled marijuana in the car but didn't see any. A drug-sniffing dog was brought, and it detected ten kilos of cocaine concealed in the rear seat upholstery. Bail for Dysmas was initially set at $5,000 but this was reduced to a $500 fine when it was determined he was just a dupe.

"It has to be cash," Dysmas said. Then, sheepishly: "Think you can get it together and come get me?"

"Of course," I assured him.

"No need to bring anyone else."

"I understand."

———•◦•———

"Has he always been unlucky?" Kat asked about Dysmas.

"I'm not sure. I think there's more to it. Something in his personality, his attitudes."

"But these recent things. Surely he couldn't foresee what happened."

"Yes, that's true. On the other hand, he was in those situations, and earlier ones, because of decisions he made in life. A chain of successive missteps."

She thought about this a moment.

"He's got you for a friend, anyway. He's lucky there."

"Well, we go way back. Before things went sour for him. Before he helped them get that way."

"Getting to be one-sided, isn't it? I mean your time, and financially, peace of mind and all. I don't mean to criticize but—"

"Yes, I know. I've thought about that. He'll have to shape up."

We fell silent. We were in her apartment, having returned from celebrating the end of our MBA studies with another couple. Kat leaned toward me, then spoke earnestly.

"I think I can help if you'll let me. If *he'll* let me."

She told me of a plan she'd envisioned earlier. It was an election year, with the stodgy Republican governor struggling in his campaign against a charismatic Democrat. The governor, in desperation, had ordered a special review of all welfare cases in the state, hoping this would enhance his image of fiscal integrity—a crusader against waste. The project required hiring an army of "case aides," paraprofessionals with limited college credits, to interview all people receiving welfare and determine their continued eligibility. Their supervisors would be current caseworkers promoted on an emergency basis. It was Kat's proposal that Dysmas be part of the influx of new state workers, gaining safe employment and structure in his life, precluding further

22

burdens on myself and our relationship. Kat herself could oversee the process from her new higher position in department management.

"You're confident it'd work?" I asked her.

"Just as long as *he's* confident and stays with it. We have to encourage him. Which mostly means you, I guess, given our situation."

"So how does he apply?"

"I have the forms. We can suggest some of the answers, but it should all be in his writing. Play up his veteran's status and puff the courses he took, never mind the grades or whether he finished. Leave out the info on that last job, just say he was traveling or doing independent study."

"A little bit true, I guess. You're a real manager now, Kat."

———◆———

The review office was one of many sprinkled throughout the state, hastily installed in whatever large indoor spaces were available. Dysmas found himself among sixty-some fellow workers, mostly new hires from the surrounding inner city. They sat in metal folding chairs at bingo tables, going though multi-page reports from welfare recipients, noting incompletions, inconsistencies, lack of verification. The newly minted supervisors looked on, occasionally checking for quality of work but hesitant to demonstrate authority. In the event of unrest they'd be vastly outnumbered by their streetwise workers. Dysmas would see one of them in the tavern he attended for lunch, just a few blocks away but across the ethnic demarcation line, unofficial but strictly observed.

The work was routine, repetitive, involving little human contact or communication, but this was to my friend's liking. He got into a groove of sorts, reporting promptly each day and going through the same required motions without significant feedback or hazards. Once the governor lost the election, however, the mood of the office changed markedly, a sense of purposelessness taking hold. A day came when the four supervisors were called into the administrator's office and came out looking confused and dejected. The project was being ignominiously ended, the case aides to be transferred to regular welfare offices, many to cover caseloads formerly served by college-degreed caseworkers. The assignments would be random for the sake of expedience.

Dysmas was soon working in an area less inner-city but still economically depressed. He had a desk set end-to-end against other desks, with wide rows of such arrangements set successively through a large open floor plan. Through a door to one side was another large area with many file cabinets and clerical staff. The other side gave access to a large area of paraprofessionals, some recycled from the review office, who had miscellaneous duties. A passageway led from there to an "intake" area at the front of the building. The intake was of new applicants, people wanting to see their caseworkers, and anyone else off the street.

My friend felt out of place as he sat at his desk, a misfit in the machine. The office had a function, he realized, and the many forms and records that appeared before him were parts of a process, something into which he was supposed to blend. There were also the phones, constantly ringing, one apiece for the five workers in his unit and another for their supervisor, who had a cubicle beside their row. Similar ringing issued from the many units surrounding their own. Dysmas was informed he was to answer his unit mates' phones as well as his own when they weren't attended, even if on a call himself. All six lines could be accessed or put on hold using lighted buttons on the phone base. It took my friend some time to get used to this since his unit mates were often away for extended times.

"Doing anything for lunch?" came a voice next to his ear.

It was Willis, a worker from the unit behind them.

"No," Dysmas answered.

"Come with Toby and me. We need three to get a table across the street."

It was a tavern kept by an elderly couple who lived in the apartment above it. They'd remained there for decades during racial change in the neighborhood.

"Twelve o'clock?" Dysmas asked.

"No, now. Beat the rush."

"I'll have to ask my supervisor."

The phones were quiet for exactly an hour from twelve to one, calls rejected at the switchboard.

"Piss on that," Willis said. "Just carry a piece of paper into the files like you're gonna look something up. Then slip out the side door with us."

Dysmas followed instructions, shielded from his supervisor's view by a stocky female unit mate working at her desk.

"That's a bitch of a unit you're in," Willis said in the pub. "Drove the worker you're replacing crazy."

"Poor Mrs. Engstrom," Toby added. "Nice fifty-something lady."

"Yeah," Willis continued. "They'd dump their own work on her and be rude about it. Twit supervisor let it slide."

The speaker was thickset and fit naturally behind a stein of beer. Toby was taller with wavy blond hair and short beard, attractive to both women and men.

"So, you come to us from a review office?" the tall one asked.

"Yeah."

"Where from before that?"

Dysmas related his taxicab experience, reluctant to mention his car delivery job, then gave a sanitized version.

"Wow, that must have been interesting," Willis remarked.

Their food arrived, cooked by the elderly wife in a tiny kitchen at the end of the bar. It was served by a woman supplementing her disability check. The menu had only a single choice but it varied by day of the week.

"Hey, Tom!" Willis shouted to the elderly barkeep. "You spike the mashed potatoes today?"

The old man ignored him.

"Never know," Willis smiled. "Might be using some of that homeboy weed."

"Nah," rejoined Toby, "even Tom wouldn't touch *that* crap. Chances are they reap it in a cemetery." Then, to Dysmas quietly:

25

"You be looking for anything like that, I'm the go-to. Anything I provide is *quality*."

They dug into their food, ordered second beers.

"Party coming up Saturday," Willis said between mouthfuls. Rachel's house. You met her yet?" he asked Dysmas. "Straight black hair, kind of loud?"

"No, afraid not."

"I'll introduce you."

"Don't worry," Toby injected. "It's not match-making. She's married."

Others were drifting into the tavern, from their office and elsewhere. One was a tall, husky man with deep-set eyes below a high receding hairline. He took a stool at the far end of the *L*-shaped bar, next to a wall.

"There's Horne," Toby observed. "Should I wave him over?"

"Hell, no!" Willis quickly answered. Then, to Dysmas: "He's in my unit. You've prob'ly heard him on the phone. What's that word—stentorian?"

"Something like that. Yeah, he's loud."

"Make a good God-the-Father someday," Toby quipped.

Dysmas had already noticed the man in the employees' parking lot, attracted by his car, a nicely kept Karmann Ghia. They'd spoken briefly about the latter, Dysmas somewhat embarrassed by his own vehicle, an old white cargo van he kept to facilitate moves. When he skipped the party that weekend, hating as he did such events, Horne told him the following week that he had done and felt the same. Dysmas sensed a commonality between them, despite the other's imposing persona. He was not surprised, therefore, when Horne asked if he'd like to drive the Karmann Ghia next weekend, himself using the old cargo van.

"I have to move some furniture for my dad's store," Horne explained. "Not real heavy stuff, mostly wood, but awkward and a lot."

Dysmas saw no reason to refuse, besides being pleased at the prospect of driving a sharp car again. The exchange took place after work that Friday with the men exchanging tips about driving their respective vehicles. Dysmas zipped off with a feeling of empowerment, wondering how he might make the most of his enhanced status. Little came to mind, however, because so many pursuits of his fellow men did not interest or even repelled him. He enjoyed driving Horne's car, at least at first, but it also made him feel like an idle, isolated man pretending to be cool. He slowed his accelerations, let his emotions subside, drove as he would in executing the most mundane of tasks. He parked the car where he could see it from his window as he mulled things over.

He phoned my apartment the next day, a Saturday, with Katerina taking the call. She alerted me to it after they'd exchanged a few words.

"He sounds excited," she said. "Better brace yourself."

Dysmas told me about the Karmann Ghia, said he'd like to take us for a drive, needing to include Kat since he knew she was with me.

"We're tied up this afternoon," I truthfully informed him. "How about this evening? We can go someplace for dinner."

He was receptive, almost enthusiastic. I still felt I had to encourage him in things, knowing his nature and not wanting to tip him into depression. He showed up promptly as dinnertime approached, then gave us a rather wild ride along Lake Shore Drive to the northern edge of the city. We had an indulgent repast at a pristine restaurant, Dysmas and Kat contending for the check while I just watched at first, then intervened and suggested a three-way split. Dysmas was rather put out, I observed. He wanted to feel like a big shot this night. When Kat suggested we tour the Baha'i Temple and Dysmas objected, opting for a disco, I went along with him. Kat looked perplexed with Dysmas so out of character, but I gave her a pronounced wink to reassure her.

It was only a short trip to Xanadu, the disco, and traffic was light, so Dysmas driving after restaurant wine was not yet an issue for us. But after we'd passed the gaudy façade and I was hit for a cover charge, I realized it was a deposit on drinks that would mostly be drunk by Dysmas. I watched from our small table as he danced with Kat, then with anonymous partners, his movements progressively wilder and seemingly out of control. He was essentially dancing and drinking by himself. His was the release and frenzy of long-suppressed emotions dating from his days of backyard trash burning. He was my opponent in the dust, the primitive and singular receiver of frustrations whom I allowed to win, would always have to help.

"Can you drive his car?" Kat finally asked me.

"Yes. I learned stick shift on a summer job."

"If he doesn't let you, I'm taking a cab."

Dysmas did take some convincing, alcohol-sodden and mentally still dancing in the chill night air, but then gave in to Kat's promise of future and greater adventures. We bundled him into the back seat where he soon lost consciousness in response to my cautious, sanely paced driving. He awoke but appeared dazed when we arrived at my building, so we led him up to my apartment to have coffee. Sitting on the couch and looking around, he asked if I had something else to drink, meaning liquor.

"The night is young," he proffered.

"Actually, Dys, it's not. We're drinking coffee now."

He gave a look that seemed uncomprehending. As Kat and I conferred by the coffeemaker, Dysmas stretched out on the couch and went to sleep. As he continued to lay still, breathing heavily for a while and finally snoring, Kat switched off the lamps, unplugged the coffeemaker, and tugged my sleeve toward the bedroom.

When we woke with the morning light, we found he was gone.

Both of us, Katerina and I, were concerned about Dysmas and hoped he was alright. Our stronger reaction to his absence, however, was relief. We realized he could be a strain on our relationship and were happy to resume our weekend without him. Kat even had me unplug the telephone. He continued to crop up in our thoughts and conversation, though, the impression of his bizarre behavior deep on our professional sensibilities.

"I think we need some distance from him," Kat said. "Deliberate, planned."

I was struck by her bluntness. My childhood friend. Yet there was no disputing the truth of her statement. I'd been gradually conditioned through the years to overlook my friend's faults, his failings, perhaps his fate.

"Maybe," I hedged. "Yes, might well be."

"We need to be more definite, Mac. It isn't as if we're a troika. You grew up with him, but I'm just a recent acquaintance that he doesn't much like."

"He's that way with all women. We've been through that."

"Well then, that's *his* problem, isn't it? Why does it have to be ours?"

She was right, I knew. There was no good explanation for the irrational bond with Dysmas I mostly just tolerated now. My relationship with her, on the other hand, was intimate and met every test of desirability. It mustn't be ruined by some hidebound wedge of obligation.

"Don't worry, Kat. I'll make him understand. From now on his involvements are his own to work out."

"Good. And thank you."

I waited uneasily for my decisive session with Dysmas, but it didn't soon arrive. He was preoccupied, on returning to work Monday, with the absence of Horne. They were to return each other's vehicles at that time, but the exchange could not take place. Dysmas was puzzled at first and restless with continued responsibility for the sports car, but the situation was soon clarified. Unusual murmurs of gossip that were spreading through the office were expressed in stark terms by Willis from the unit behind.

"Yeah, he got arrested for rape. He's sitting in the county jail."

It had apparently been reported on the evening news, briefly amidst the politics, celebrities, and usual shootings. A mugshot of Horne glowering had been shown.

"When was it?" Dysmas asked.

"Saturday night. Lured a fifteen-year-old girl into a van he had. Someone walking by heard her screams."

Lunchtime in the bar saw Willis's table bothered by other patrons seeking news about Horne. They fell back when Toby expressed irritation, but he was ineffective against a plainclothes policeman backed by two in uniform. Plainclothes produced a warrant for the arrest of Dysmas on suspicion of being an accessory to rape. A motor vehicle check had listed him as owner of the van used by Horne in commission of his crime. Dysmas tried to explain about the trade, Horne's given reason for it, but the police essentially told him to save it for the judge. Perhaps due to the surrounding crowd they refrained from placing him in handcuffs.

Dysmas was later cleared when Katerina and I supported his alibi for Saturday night, as well as his motivation in agreeing to the trade. There were still repercussions for my friend, unfortunately. Horne's action had besmirched the image of the public aid department, its administrators unforgiving since it reflected on themselves. Dysmas was seen as having helped cause the problem, his face appearing next to Horne's in news reports. As still a probationary employee, he did not have full civil service protection. He could therefore be dismissed for "generally unsatisfactory performance." This is indeed what happened. Dysmas received his old van back after it was processed as evidence, but the Karmann Ghia disappeared after sitting two nights in the employees' parking lot, apparently stolen.

Of much greater consequence, from my perspective, were the results for Kat. Thanks to her assistance and support for Dysmas, and his ignominious fate, she too was tarnished by the scandal. In a meeting with the regional administrator, she was told that she was being transferred to another region in the state by order of their department director, who answered only to the governor. Kat's new workplace was about three hundred miles away in an area mostly rural. She saw the transfer as clearly punitive, but on her management level she had no alternative short of resigning. That was something she was not prepared to do, her career taking precedence over her ties to the city, which sadly included myself.

3.

Dysmas was not oblivious to the pathos in his life, and he vaguely saw that he had helped create it. While others had done him wrong or shown indifference, it was usually his own decisions that placed him in those situations. He could not stand to continue along an archipelago of blunders. In reviewing events, it occurred to him to reach back to an early decision of his that had been frustrated, a course not followed. If his parents had not ignorantly blocked his entry into the religious life, all would have different and he might be living happily. The priesthood, of course, was long gone as an option, but there were orders of religious brothers or monks that accepted late or delayed vocations. A call to the local parish office put him in touch with a few, one of which appealed to him for its isolated location, something he thought he'd find therapeutic.

The Order of the Sacred Virgin was located two states to the west, across countless cornfields, grasslands, and rough terrain. Dysmas was met at the train station by a handyman from the monastery driving an old pickup truck. They drove for some time along mostly deserted roads, turning finally into a hardly noticeable opening in a grove beside the road. A winding cinder drive through nondescript overgrowth brought them to a fort-like stone structure topped by a single cross. There was no identifying sign. As the handyman cut the engine and moved to exit the truck, a pair of cowled monks approached from one side of the entrance doors. Dysmas awaited their welcome, and his destiny.

The seasons were slowly passing. For many months Dysmas had climbed the stone stairways, sung hymns in the gloomy chapel, and watched the birds as they pecked in the courtyard. He'd see them converse and fly about, and he'd remember doing such things himself. He could do them again if he wished, but he chose to stay here.

Walking the garden path, he breathed fecundity. A wind was blowing through the vines, reminding him that he wasn't very young now. He'd slowed the pace of his life—that was clear to him—but it still would pass quickly and someday would end. His robe would grow heavy on him and the shadow in which he lived would deepen. He'd drift with the years until he was beyond humanity. It wasn't quite what he'd wanted, but there was just this one way for him, as there should be just one for any person.

"Life here is hard," Superior had said to him.

"Then it's what I need."

"Our only comfort is prayer."

"It will be my support, my source of strength."

Superior hesitated, perhaps dubious.

"In time, you'll grow used to the routine."

He came to the end of the garden, exited through an iron gate. Branches rustled and crickets chirped as he entered the forest. He felt slow and awkward, but he'd come this way often and his sandals gripped the earth with certainty. He'd see the same trees, hear the same birds whenever he went to meet her, she who was always there. He found her this day with a sunray on her brow, leaving him with a sense of emptiness about to be filled. She smiled beneath her veil and he was overcome with love. He fell to his knees and bowed to her, separated by a little pond. She guarded this pond day and night; he filled it when the water went low. To honor her, he'd gather pebbles and toss them gently into the pond. With each little splash, a burst of love would thrill his heart, partly subsiding as ripples ran over the pond. When the last ripple had died and fulfillment was achieved, he'd raise his eyes and sit limply on the ground. He didn't care what happened next.

"She's a paragon of virtue," he'd been told.

"So in loving her we love virtue?"

"No. In loving her we love divinity."

As he moved around the pond, he marveled at the perfection of this woman. He'd met many others in his life, yet nowhere had he met this actual love. Love for him had to be complete, perfect, to exist at all. The other women, people he hardly remembered now, were lonely and frightened creatures who gave of themselves only to achieve something. And their goals were shallow, silly, yet they debased themselves for them. It was absurd. Only here had he found a woman at peace, who could give without object and be greater for it. Taking her hands, he leaned forward and kissed her sacred heart.

After a while, he knew it was time to go. A wind was rising and it was growing cool, the little pond was shimmering, and the woman withdrawing into shadow. He kissed her one last time and she smiled as he backed away, retreating into the haze of promises. Would it rain tonight? Would he live to see the sunrise, await the setting? Separation was always such a risk. Why couldn't we just stay where we belonged and never move?

"We all have our work to do, Brother Dysmas."

He walked slowly, unwillingly, through the forest as startled inhabitants scurried about. This was the greatest meaning: the world away from words. The eternity of the woods, its smells and sounds, were at the core of every human being. To shed the trappings of culture was to join the real world as one. This was his destiny, he thought, and he was thankful for it.

There was a sound. He stopped.

It was a sound somehow familiar, a groan or low squeal, soft and yet distinct in the dark colors of the forest. He thought for a minute. Perhaps it was something giving birth. He should continue on his way, he knew, but he also knew that he was one with the forest and had shared his secrets with it. He was a part of the forest like the plants and animals and it should have no secrets from him. As he moved away from the path, picking his way carefully, his mind grew silent in anticipation. With each step or move of a branch, he listened for another sound. And once or twice more he heard it, the tiny grunt or muffled cry. When he was close to where the other must be, he squatted and waited before parting the bushes. And again it came: a tiny bark and faint rustling against the grass and ground. Reaching forward with the strength that was his faith, he pushed aside the leaves and gazed upon creation.

A young man, nude, hovered over a prone young woman, also nude. Her hair was long, golden brown, and she writhed beneath his caresses. He kissed and nibbled at her, her body arching off the ground. It arched like the Savior on the cross, eyes toward heaven and lips parted in agony, entreaty. Dysmas would watch in the chapel as dusty sunrays caressed His body. If only he could take Him down and relieve His suffering, hold the ravaged body and comfort the God-made-man. But no, all he could do was kneel and yearn, crouch and watch with passion as he did now in the bushes with damp earth beneath. The young people before him were enthralled by their passion. Their hair gently fluttered in a rising wind and her hands wandered wistfully on his back. Dysmas was sweating in his heavy robe, watching in awe as the union of bodies was achieved before him. He forgot his own presence, totally enraptured in the dying light of day. Only when climax was achieved did he remember his soul, his need to get away. Withdrawing as slowly as he could, letting no swinging branch announce his presence, he returned to his path and stumbled home in shame.

He was late for vespers that night, slipping into the rearmost pew. He should feel safe here, he knew, inhaling the scent of wood and incense, but the rows of anointed heads seemed to chastise him. They were like great unblinking eyes admonishing him for his sins, the lowered hoods like shields against his arguments. Was he worthy of them? Did he merit his place in this temple of self-sacrifice? He didn't know. All he knew was that he once had been evil, that his life and ways had been wrong and he now must atone for them. It was what he deserved, what he needed and wanted, and nothing should interfere. His new attitude must be preserved against the rotten charms of sin. It was precious, after all, as a state of mind—both a means and an end. It had freed him from the gutter of perverted dreams.

As he went about his chores, he often had to catch himself from sliding back. He tried to be always aware of his new state, but he was often drawn toward idleness, lust, and contempt. These were now his adversaries, powerful lures that tested his faith. They had a purpose, therefore, and he understood this, but he wished they would atrophy, disappear. He couldn't make this happen, he felt, because he lacked a quality that was only found in a holy, virginal woman, the mother of divinity. He could never add this grace to his faith, but he could come as close as possible through pure, nympholeptic yearning that would prove his intent to himself and God. His weakness would be absolved then, and he'd be given strength to endure.

The couple in the woods had disrupted Dysmas's new life. It wasn't that he envied them, desiring their debauchery, and it wasn't that they angered him. It was simply that the image of them was fixed in his mind, filling a great space and making it hard to think of other things. They were there like some giant, tasteless sculpture, cluttering and defiling the vestibule of his temple. No more could he offer the litany of praise that was his link to the spiritual world, for this monstrosity made it desecration. Being so close to evil, he felt, was like being part of it. It warped or sullied everything you did, so you could only be good or happy again by breaking from it, putting some distance between it and yourself. Now this wasn't so hard when the evil was concrete, confined by boundaries in space and time. But when it was internal—an obscene image forcing itself on you—how could you separate from it? His usual recourse was prayer, but his prayers were tainted now by the monster in his vestibule. He couldn't expect they'd be answered. No, some sort of atonement was necessary. He wasn't sure how to achieve it, but knew he'd find the answer where he'd found his answers before. He'd see her that evening, as he always did, and she'd tell him what to do.

He took a new route this time, leaving the familiar path to avoid where he'd heard the young couple. The thickets were hard to penetrate, and some had thorns, but his robe was armor and he plodded on. As he neared the sacred clearing, the shrine that housed his eternal woman, there was a cry and he stopped to listen. He heard a squeal of pleasure, then laughter, the voices of a man and a woman. Could it be them? At the shrine itself? It just couldn't be, he thought. Pushing aside rough, wild branches, he forged through the forest, racing against the surging panic. When he came to the spot, the bubble in time where all his hopes were stored, he hung at the edge of the spectacle before him.

They were naked in the pond, frolicking, the sacred water trickling over their bodies as they splashed. Dysmas wasn't seen at first, his rage mounting uncontrollably. When it finally exploded it propelled him in a savage charge toward the young couple.

"Desecrators! Agents of Satan!"

They froze in their play, staring at the monk-robed lunatic that was bearing down on them. The girl cringed away but the boy stood his ground, extending a hand as if to placate a dog. The water on their bodies would be cold, their flesh feeling like clay, already dead.

"To purge the temple of my faith, the Lord will smite His enemies!"

Lunging past the extended hand, Dysmas rammed his fist into the boy's stomach. The boy slumped toward the water, was caught in angry arms, went hurtling out of the pond. He lay moaning on the grass as the girl cried for mercy. Dysmas ignored her.

"Vile, infectious vermin! Punishment is my duty, my honor!"

Pouncing on his victim, the monk pummeled cruelly, quelling the boy's resistance. But the rage was far from satisfied. Rising slowly over his foe, Dysmas turned his eyes to the holy mother.

"Show me the way, my queen."

He followed her gaze across the clearing, saw the naked girl. She was cowering, shivering in the light breeze of evening. As he edged toward her, the girl's eyes went wide, unblinking. She was a frightened doe, innocent perhaps but the instrument of atonement.

"No! Please!"

She fell to her knees, started to cry. Sweating and breathing heavily, Dysmas still approached.

"Please, don't hurt me. Please don't."

He came and gripped her arm, the forbidden flesh of woman. Her muscles were supple, the skin smooth. She trembled and stared at his hand.

"Oh, God. Oh, *God!*"

Reaching back, he slapped her across the face and released her. She fell back on the grass and lay sobbing.

"Blasphemer! You must know His glory, His kingdom and its power! I'll set you on His altar this very night!"

She was pulling her knees into her chest. But he was used to heavy loads and picked her up easily, flinging her over his shoulder like a sack of potatoes. She squirmed and tried to break free, but he tightened his grip and kept his balance. His mind was filled with knowledge of his purpose: to bring this woman to the altar of God. Plodding forward, he murmured prayers and exaltations to force off invading distractions. His was a mission based on a sacred pact, and the legions of hell must not interfere.

Nonetheless, as he strode through the forest with the girl on his back, there were inroads by the demon Satan. The smallness and softness of her body, its dampness and smell, were things he could not escape. The image of her nakedness floated into his mind, glowed through the fog like a radiant crucifix. He was already warm from carrying her, but the thought of her body made him hotter. He would struggle, wrestling with the shadow of his soul, and his grip on the girl would tighten until she cried out. The demon's spell would be broken then and Dysmas's pace would quicken, the map of his pilgrimage clear once more.

"Where are you taking me?"

He did not respond.

"We meant no harm. Please let me go."

"Silence, harlot!"

She was quiet then, resigned to her fate, and rode his shoulder in horror. There was no sound except the branches that swept over her body. He was strong but awkward, she must have thought, like he was drunk. Maybe he was crazy. He could hurt her if he wished so she had to cooperate until she could get away.

"Begone, Satan! Out with your poisonous thoughts!"

Dysmas was hot and wet, the girl grown clammy. Night was falling and the crickets chirped louder. The trees thinned and soon they were in the monastery garden, the girl looking desperately about. There were buildings and maybe movement at a window, but she couldn't be sure and so didn't call out. Dysmas trod slowly, picking his way up the garden path, then passed through a creaky door. The hallway inside was of stone and lit by candles. Dysmas raised loud sandy scrapes as his sandals met the stones. They passed a kitchen where another monk was working, but he didn't look up and the girl was reluctant to shout. There was stone all around and an angry heave would have hurt her badly.

There were voices from somewhere, low but excited.

Dysmas was climbing some stairs, old and worn though made of stone. He was tired and paused on each step. The voices came during the intervals, resonant from up ahead, from an intersecting passage. His pace quickened with the stairs behind him but slowed to a halt when he noticed men watching. They were silent and unmoving, waiting for Dysmas to come to them.

"Brother Dysmas—" one of them began.

But he brushed right by and tightened his grip on the girl. They were two more monks, dressed the same as Dysmas but smaller. The girl renewed her struggles as she passed them.

Dysmas kept going, lumbering toward his goal. Someone got in his way and was knocked down. It was another monk, cringing as they passed him. There was a turn and they entered the chapel, a large one with many candles. There were statues of saints and a strong, sweet smell. There were two more monks at the altar, one looking back at Dysmas. The second monk also took notice and they moved to protect the altar.

"Come no closer, brother!"

But he charged at them in the flickering light. He was soaked with sweat and panting, but the challenge gave him new strength. The air was heavy and there was no escape; he'd bring the girl to the altar or die trying. The monks in front braced for the onslaught. They were fearful but dedicated, ready for combat in defense of the sanctuary. As Dysmas charged them, he saw that they didn't have a chance. Smiling broadly, about to laugh, he plowed into them with elbows high. They flew away as he roared in triumph. Stumbling over the altar steps, he dropped his captive at the foot of the great cross.

The girl was stunned a moment, then saw she was free. Above her was the Savior with paint chipping off his knees. Monks were running up from all directions, robes sweeping the air around shaven heads. Dysmas swung wildly at them, knocking them back and bellowing with gusto. The altar was engulfed by robes, the community converging on its errant member. Swinging in all directions, feeling the mob press closer, Dysmas lost his balance and fell back on the steps. The surge of monks swept over him, drowning his rage in a sea of piety.

When he came to his senses, he found himself in a little room that served as the infirmary. He'd often passed this room and wished he could rest in it, withdraw from his chores and lie in bed while others attended to him. But he'd always caught himself, kept his belief that he should work hard and serve. There were two little windows in this room and, standing on the bed, he could see into the courtyard. The birds were there, pecking at pebbles, the first light of day giving color to the monastery. It was quiet, but a sense of urgency lingered in the air. Lowering himself, he knelt by the bed and lost himself in prayer. It was easy now to pray; the monster was gone from his vestibule.

There was a brief knock. The superior came in.

"Good morning, Brother Dysmas."

He left the door open and drew up a chair.

"We must talk."

"Yes, I know."

"The police were here. The young man is in the hospital."

"It's a grievous sin that I've committed."

"You can only gain forgiveness from God, whom you've offended."

"Yes."

"But there's more to this, brother—a decision that I've had to make."

"A decision?"

"Regarding yourself. And the Order."

Dysmas was stunned, but the superior's expression was firm.

"Yes, I understand."

He was told of a call to his emergency contact, which was me, and my agreement to house him temporarily, assist him in finding useful occupation.

"Our prayers will follow you. If you like, I can provide a recommendation."

"Thank you, Superior."

But he needed no recommendation. He knew very well whom he'd seek for assistance. She needn't be found only in the woods, in a little shrine that was now defiled. He could find her in all the great cities, and in many small towns. Whatever form she took, he'd know her by a certain eternal beauty, the warmth of her caring. When he was with her, he'd be strengthened against all that was wasteful or corrupt. He wouldn't need those things, so he wouldn't need to fear them. He'd only need her, his caring woman, and he'd honor her with the strength she gave him.

He waited as the superior left, then went to collect his things. He laid his robe over the back of a hard wooden chair. This raised some dust, swirling in a shaft of sunlight. Dysmas watched it, thinking of how he'd slept here for many months, the austerity of it all. It was good that he was leaving, he thought, both bad and good. But that's how most things were.

4.

I'd expected Dysmas to be disconsolate when he arrived, but his demeanor instead suggested a vague sort of optimism. He was reluctant, of course, to relate the details of his departure from the monastery, but they inevitably came out in our discussions over the next couple of days. I could put him up briefly but more permanent plans would have to be made. His apparent optimism, his unswerving trust in my judgment, implied a dependence growing out of delusion. I secretly hoped that the religious life had not left too heavy an imprint on his psyche.

I'd tried to begin preparing for my friend soon after hearing from his superior. The obvious needs for shelter and work shared the focus of my efforts, but I was ill-prepared to seek these for another person. Fortunately, I'd nurtured a relationship with a woman in the real estate section of our private equity firm, and she assisted me. Our personal relationship was a secret from the firm, since intraoffice romance was frowned upon by high execs, but we could discuss Dysmas under the guise of business.

"There are vacancies in several of the properties," Sheila said to me at her desk, "but there's one that might meet both his needs."

"Oh? How's that?"

"It's an opening for resident manager. Thirty apartments over five entrances around a narrow courtyard. The twelve apartments in front are one bedrooms, the rest are studios. One of the apartments in front is retrofitted with a small office. That's where he'd live. A resident janitor lives in one of the studios. Think your guy is up to it?"

I briefly reflected, decided he'd have to be.

"Sure. Might need a little support. He'd have my number, be free to call me."

"Good. Any contracting out, of course, has to come through us here."

"I take it this is an older building."

"Yes, in Uptown. Not a bad neighborhood, really. Sort of 'in transition.' Moving toward gentrification."

She gave me an inquisitive look, slightly smiling beneath her blond hair tied back.

"You're quite a friend to this guy, Mac."

"It's just we go back a long way. Some friendships you go through and they're done, others stick around. Even if you're not real close."

"Like with a relative. Like he's a brother, maybe."

"Yeah. A brother in dust."

Sheila hesitated, then: "I'll take that on faith."

———◦———

The Wayside Market, where Dysmas did his shopping, had a yogurt bar just bigger than a phone booth. All the produce was organically grown, there were no cigarettes, and yet one of the narrow aisles was entirely wines and beers. Coming from the monastery, Dysmas's tastes were simple and his shopping easily done. He had a feeling, though, as he squeezed through the little store, that others were shopping here for exciting, sublime ways of life.

The market was only a block from his apartment building, in which one of the checkout girls also lived. He'd see her on the street sometimes with books in her arms and assumed she attended the neighborhood university. She was pretty, with soft raven hair and olive complexion, reminding him somewhat of his Madonna in the forest. He'd greet her warmly and she wasn't suspicious of him since he was the building manager. She expected him to know her name, he thought, but he didn't know the given one. Just her initial: C. This was on her mailbox, which didn't often appear to have mail in it.

"Do they have any celery seed dressing?" he asked her.

"Middle aisle, near the back."

He already knew it was there. He'd just seen it. He'd been looking for something less ordinary to ask her about.

"I've never had it," he said. "I was thinking of trying something new."

She smiled, her brown eyes reflecting the ceiling lights.

"Really? I'd say that's great!"

Dysmas felt encouraged. He faked a move to leave, stopping decisively.

"By the way. This may sound strange, but I don't know your first name."

"It's Camille. Isn't that in your records?"

She sounded worried. Being in the records was important, apparently. Then he remembered she was a college student.

"Most of the records are downtown. All I had was your initial."

He felt like saying something more, something endearing, but nothing came to mind.

"Well," she said, "now you can put my name in."

And she turned to check out a customer. Dysmas left for the salad dressing, obliged to buy it to cover his ploy.

Camille's apartment, like Dysmas's, was on the bottom of three floors in the old courtyard building. She lived at the middle entrance, Dysmas at the front with windows facing the central walkway. He thus got an oblique view of her front window. He could rarely see her, but he could see her lights and her shadow moving about. Knowing she was a student, he knew he shouldn't disrupt her studying. But from the movement of her shadow he guessed when she did other things, assuming she didn't move while studying. He had to go see her, he felt, since they couldn't talk in the store and the street was undependable. He wanted to ask her out, get some time alone with her. He wasn't still a monk, after all.

She opened her door at once, showing no surprise. She was wearing a Mickey Mouse tee shirt with nothing under it.

"The reason I came over," Dysmas said, "is that—well, I was going to the film fest at the Monitor. There's a Mexican film tonight, avant-garde, by a famous director down there. I was wondering if you'd like to come along."

It seemed to take forever to say it, Dysmas refraining from looking down at Mickey Mouse while Camille tilted her head, listening.

"I'd like to," she said. "Really, I would. Only thing is, I've got these exams."

She gestured at some books and things on her table. Dysmas gazed at them, grateful for a place to turn his eyes. Camille was watching him, waiting for him to say something, but he didn't know what to say now. He still wanted to be with her. He smiled, his store-customer smile, and she seemed to like it.

"Tell you what," she said. "Why don't we have a drink together later?"

"At the Leather Bottle?"

"No, here."

"All right. What time?"

"Next Wednesday. Say, sevenish?"

It was Friday evening. Dysmas began to calculate the time until the rendezvous, but Camille's eyes were sparkling. He was supposed to say something, but was she joking or serious?

"How does that sound to you?" Camille prompted.

"Oh, fine."

"So what do you like to drink?"

He studied the glow of soft lighting on her olive skin.

"The one with olives—what's it called?"

"Martinis. I guess you don't drink much. I'll have to make them weak."

"No, make them strong."

"Why?"

"Well, I'm kind of big. A weak drink doesn't do much for me."

"Okay. But, you know, maybe you should go out more. You don't have to live like a monk here just because you're building manager."

He was still smiling when she closed the door, but then his face twitched and he let it sag. So he *was* still a monk, after all. He must have looked like an oaf, he thought, but she'd been awfully nice about it. He'd enjoy thinking of her during the movie, which he had to attend to cover another ploy.

He avoided the store that weekend, and Monday and Tuesday as well. It was important that she not change her mind about Wednesday, so he mustn't give her cause. It was foolishness, he knew, but this waiting for Wednesday wasn't his idea. She had reasons, apparently, so he had to adjust as best he could.

"I haven't seen you at the store," she said.

"Well, I was pretty well stocked."

"Filling up on celery seed?"

"It does a lot for cucumbers. I'll have to try it on bean sprouts."

She smiled and sipped her martini. She seemed to relax as they talked, though to Dysmas his comments sounded stupid. She seemed to like him and he wondered why.

"I suppose you know I was in a religious order."

"No, I didn't know."

"Your comment last week, about my living like a monk—it made me think you knew."

"No. Honestly, I didn't. How long have you been out? A civilian, I mean."

"Just a few weeks. A friend helped me get this job. Wouldn't have gotten it on my own."

"I'm glad you came. Truth is, I didn't notice you much at first, shopping there at the market. As I listen to you, though—your ways— it makes me think you're someone I can really like."

Dysmas was taken by surprise and stared at her. He drained his martini. She watched him do it, giving him a wink. But she didn't offer another drink that night, mentioning some schoolwork. It wasn't yet nine when Dysmas departed, the single martini a long-past source of warmth.

"Won't you eat your olive?" she'd asked.

Dysmas consumed it.

"I always eat them," she said. "It's like punctuation, in a way."

He glanced toward the door.

"I'd like to see you again," he said. "On a personal basis, I mean. Perhaps—"

"How about next Wednesday?"

He'd been about to mention the film fest, still in progress.

"Well, sure. Maybe we can—"

"We'll have two martinis each, double our consumption. And you can tell me more about your life in the monastery."

"If you like."

Her smile sealed it. He bumbled out the door, pleased but vaguely disturbed by his easy success. Things should come harder, he thought, but maybe that was just his monk mentality. He tried to avoid the thought in the intervening week, concentrating instead on their second rendezvous. He went to the market once, needing to see her as well as to buy his groceries. He bought a lot, including bean sprouts, to minimize his shopping trips. He might still blow it all, he thought, with some clumsy action or comment.

When she made the next martinis, they were stronger as well as more numerous.

"We can handle them," she said. "Last week was easy."

She was even more relaxed this time, lying back like a princess as she laughed at his stories of his brother monks. He attributed this to the drinks. He felt them himself as he viewed the contours within her tee-shirt. It was *Save the Whales* this time.

At nine-thirty, she said she had a term paper to finish.

"We'll do it again next week," she said. "Three apiece then, Dysmas."

He agreed and left, feeling he was blessed by Providence. Why, he thought, argue with success? Were not the greatest blessings in life mysteries that transcended our understanding? He fell asleep quickly with these thoughts, launched into another week of waiting. Sailing was smooth, however, and he resumed his normal shopping habits. He even threw away the celery seed dressing.

On the third Wednesday, she had six martinis lined up in her refrigerator. She didn't wear a tee-shirt this time, but a transparent blouse with frills—also with nothing underneath, however. Dysmas couldn't look at her during the first drink, with Camille eyeing him coyly, seeming to enjoy his shyness. Dysmas wasn't bothered, though, knowing there were two drinks to go, and sure enough his second changed things. He looked her in the eyes, his peripheral vision sensing the rest of her, then dropped his gaze whenever she looked away. They had their third drinks slowly, Camille becoming sleepy, and Dysmas studied her without inhibition. He noted every detail, their enhancement by the frilly blouse. He would later feel foolish about this.

"Exam this week," she mumbled. "Come again Wednesday. We'll do something then, I think."

Despite his drinking, Dysmas was thrilled by the prospect. He touched her shoulder as he moved to leave, but she gently put his hand away.

"Next week," she said.

And there was the smile—woozy but alluring, he thought. It promised the enchantment enjoyed by his fellow patrons of the Wayside Market.

She wore a dress next time, and black stockings. Dysmas found her formal, especially when he saw the five martinis on a silver tray.

"Two and a half each," she explained. "The three were a bit much last time."

"How do we handle the halves?"

"After we each have two, we won't mind sharing a glass."

"I wouldn't mind now."

It just came out of him—seemed harmless—but he saw he shouldn't have said it. Her eyes looked up as she sipped her drink, a mild reproach. The ground rules were set, the ritual had to be observed. It was beyond the questioning stage, the negotiating. And this was the night they would do something.

"There are some things about me you should know," she said. "See, I'm not from around here."

"That's all right. Neither am I."

"Yes, you've told me. But your reasons aren't unusual. I mean, they're acceptable."

To Dysmas, getting booted from the monastery had seemed unique, and he still felt a cloud of shame about it. But Camille had her own perspective, he knew. The important thing now was that nothing interfere with *them*.

"Whatever your past," he said, "I accept you. This is the present, a new time, and I really think that—well, we belong together."

She smiled and looked into her drink. They never had the fifth one, though. It remained on the silver tray as she asked him to wait another week. She seemed reserved, more formal again, despite the two martinis in her. Dysmas agreed, of course.

He again avoided the Wayside Market, uneasy now and unsure what to do. Most important, he thought, was to not lose ground. So he waited for Wednesday and went to her door as usual, his mouth anticipating martinis. He found Camille in her jeans and a sweatshirt, no picture or slogan on it. The drinks were all made, one with two olives in it.

"That's the fifth," she explained. "The big one."

She made a point, he thought, of being informal this time. She lay on her couch and pumped him for stories of the monks, laughing heartily whether they were funny or not. But then, he noticed, she'd made the drinks stronger than usual.

"We're getting down to the last one," he said.

"No, that's for later. To celebrate, or maybe to drown our sorrows. See, up to now I've needed these for courage. You maybe thought *you* did, but I needed them more."

He waited, letting her build her courage. But her eyes were suddenly sad and she looked at him almost accusingly.

"It isn't a question of innocence," she said. "I'm certainly not innocent. But there's a need to get out of something that's trapped me. It's in my way as a woman and a young person. I needed to recreate it, live it through, defeat it this time. I need to break through, to smash the stigma and show how my sex is still pure. And it *is* pure, I know!"

She sat up suddenly and beamed, all sadness gone from her olive features.

"Let's do it, Dysmas! Now!"

Her raven hair swirled as she wrestled out of her sweatshirt. There was nothing underneath and Dysmas was confused, mentally struggling to fit this in with his impressions of her—his Madonna, his female Savior. Both of them were standing now. Camille stood smiling, a soft amber glow on the contours of her body. The glow shifted with her

48

breathing, deep now, and Dysmas felt magnetized. He moved slowly forward, his mind blank, his hands rising to hold her.

There was a tremor in her, which he found pleasing, and a twitch in her smile that he sought to calm. But as his hands rose to her body the shaking increased. As he touched the olive skin, the trembling became violent and her smile was a grimace, unkissable. His attraction to her was cancelled and he stepped back in shock. She was holding her arms tightly but the rest of her body shook uncontrollably. She dropped to the couch and pressed her knees together, the shaking restrained but still raging. Needing to react, Dysmas reached for her sweatshirt and fumbled to pull it over her. Camille didn't speak—couldn't, it seemed—until she was covered. Even then the trembling continued, in spasms now.

"It was on a Wednesday they came," she said, "the night that used to be the nicest."

"Who?"

"My father and his friend. It was Dad's night off. Always it was Wednesday. And before my mom died it was a special time—our special meal, talking together, games. No visitors like the weekend, just family. But then it was all different. My father changed, became bitter and hateful, blamed *me* for everything."

She wasn't crying, just looking straight ahead. Her voice occasionally quavered from the shaking.

"So, then something happened?" Dysmas pried.

"They'd been drinking downstairs. Using some drugs, too. The friend brought them over. I heard them on the stairs, wondered why they both were coming up. Then when my door opened and I saw their faces, I somehow knew. So unthinkable before. My father held me down, took from me all that was left in my heart for him, for men in general, for life. I wanted to die that night but I'd never thought about it before so I didn't know what to do. I just suffered, denied, then slipped out in the morning. I felt like an animal, a lost dog."

"Where did you go?"

"An aunt took care of me, helped me recover. Except, as you see, there's no recovering."

Dysmas felt powerless. What could he possibly do for this girl? He was a cause of pain to her, maybe had been from the beginning. And she could have little to offer *him*, it seemed.

"I'm sorry," he said, "but why did you let our meetings go on?"

"I was lonely, wanted to see someone. But I insisted on Wednesday—the special day—so I'd be on my guard, remembering the other time. But as it went on, Dysmas, I thought I could let go, erase that other Wednesday with a new one, where sex was wonderful instead of terrible. I thought I could live then like those people who come in the store. They seem to have interesting, exciting lives with nothing holding them back."

"Yes, I thought of that myself."

"Did you? Oh, and you thought that by going with me—"

Dysmas saw the irony emerging, perhaps absurdity, hoped she wouldn't laugh. He needed to change the subject.

"We still have the one with two olives," he said, and rose to get the last martini.

But Camille caught his arm.

"No," she said. "We shouldn't drink that one."

"Why not?"

"It's poisoned."

He sat back down.

"You see," she said, "after that other Wednesday—the bad one—I continued to think about suicide. But it didn't seem right, just ending it all in defeat. Then when I thought I could erase that night, doing it with you, I got this crazy idea I should end things right after. Forever. It would keep things from changing back again, collapsing into evil. I wasn't sure I'd be going through with it, but it seemed to make sense so I made the special drink."

"Was it ready last week, too?"

"Yes, taped to the silver tray. That way you wouldn't choose it over the others. But this week I thought the two olives were better. I mean, until I saw that everything was wrong."

She dropped her eyes contritely. Dysmas, his thinking confused, fell back on his emotions. He found that he wasn't angry, that even now he felt tender toward Camille.

"Thanks for warning me," he said.

She smiled, appearing relieved, and he saw that she'd stopped shaking. The evil had passed for now, it seemed.

"If you still want to," she said, "maybe we can still catch a movie. Only not tonight, and never on Wednesdays anymore."

"Sure," Dysmas responded. "That'll be nice."

5.

Amid the many issues that Dysmas encountered in managing the apartment building, the furniture stripper seemed a saving grace. He was bronze and gleaming as he toiled out in the courtyard under the declining sun. That was shortly after he'd moved in. They had only a brief exchange that time, the first since Dysmas had given Robert the keys, but it was pleasant. As the manager departed, he was conscious of charm and creativity. This tenant was somehow beautiful, he thought, and apart from the hard-charging horde.

His name, Robert Duggan, seemed an understatement. With his tall, lithe frame, handsome face, and neatly styled hair, he should have been called something fancier, musical. He lived in one of the best apartments, a one-bedroom fronting the street on the top floor. He never even asked about the studios or lower-priced one-bedrooms. He dressed well, too—fashionably and without gaudiness. But in less visible ways he was economical, refurbishing old furniture and using generic laundry detergent. His tastes were simple, it seemed, despite his elegant bearing.

"Like some tea?" he asked Dysmas one day. "Plain old Lipton, I'm afraid."

Dysmas accepted. Robert had been coming from the laundry room and, on meeting Dysmas, had stopped to converse at length. It was as if he'd been longing for a listener, Dysmas thought, and perhaps a friend.

"I've started a poem," Robert said in his apartment. "That's something new for me."

"You're a writer, then?"

"Free-lance creative. Props, displays, promotions of all sorts. But this is a personal thing apart from work—the essence of expression, hopefully."

"You'll send it to magazines when you're finished?"

"It's not that kind of poem. It's an epic, my own conception—a book length work in the Homeric tradition."

"What's it about?"

Robert smiled gratefully and gazed out the windows, which were veiled by hanging plants.

"A satanist," he replied, "but he's not one by choice."

"Brainwashed?"

"Nothing epic about *that*. No, he's set on his course by conflicting forces in early life, and the futility of dealing with things at home."

"Bad family life?"

"Maybe not for everyone. But for a sensitive, intelligent child, there isn't much to gain from a frequently absent father and religious fanatic of a mother. No problem-solving, no social skills—just isolation and guilt. He's insecure and wets the bed. But that, they say, is the devil in him."

His look was far away, his tea forgotten. Dysmas saw a melancholy depth in Robert's youth. He didn't want to hurt this boy, say anything wrong.

"He had no one, then?"

Robert suddenly smiled.

"Oh, he does! His adoring godmother, single by nature, who encourages him against the world. She's that way herself, you see, a person of challenging opinions, with a weakness for horoscopes and psychic phenomena."

"This led to his getting into satanism?"

"No, not so much. But it shields him in his isolation. He spends tons of time reading, or doing homework, trying to perfect it. Kids his age dislike him, of course, until he meets the *contact*.

"A satanist?"

"A cell member, yes."

"Didn't the godmother help him?"

"She sees him less often with his growing isolation. He sees her boyfriend more, actually—a postman who starts him into stamp collecting."

"So then what happened?"

"That's as far as I've gotten, for now. See, I'm taking great care in doing the beginning, making it one that hooks the reader—or listener, since it's a poem—into the circle, the mind, the feelings of the boy. It's inevitable that he becomes a satanist. That has to be understood."

"Of course."

Robert looked away from him. Dysmas relaxed amid wooden furniture, oriental rugs, and aquariums that glinted and gurgled. The bronzed young man belonged in the sun, it seemed, yet this was where he freed his imagination. His movements in the courtyard were smooth, controlled. His life out there was for public consumption, a trade of labor for his secret sensitivity, a silent dwelling on past tragedies. He'd chosen to share it with Dysmas and the manager felt appreciative, curious for more.

Robert's visitors, to Dysmas, were high-class people. Well-dressed and mannered like Robert himself, they would come in twos and threes and depart at early hours. An exception was a pale young woman who would hang about the courtyard if Robert wasn't home and wait for him. When Dysmas asked about her, Robert said she was his sister.

"Why does she loiter outside so long?"

"She has problems. Emotional. Goes back a long time."

He didn't want to discuss her, Dysmas thought.

"So, how's your poem coming?"

"The epic? It's coming hard, Dysmas. With difficulty. Not the rough, outward story. It's the limitations of language that hurt—constrain the expression of a boy's feelings, his greatly changed perceptions and relationship with reality."

"This resulted from contact with the satanist?"

"No, it's what *causes* the contact, I mean his reciprocating. See, most of his peers, as a teenager, are very cruel to him. The girls see him as a nerd, the boys as someone to mock. Even adults pick up on it. People at a summer job, a coach when he goes out for track—trying to change himself and seeing it backfire—and then his parents. His father, home from sales trips, wonders why he's not into sports. His mother, despite her religiousness, wants him to be popular with girls.

54

"So, it was only his godmother he could go to."

"Yes, when she isn't busy with the postman. But this other boy, the contact, is someone he sees every day. The contact shows him literature—LaVey's book, other stuff—and it seems okay because his godmother is offbeat, too. The boy meets the cell members and they bomb him with love, give him things. There's even girls, sex. They do it in front of a video camera but the boy can't resist. The cell gives him jobs to do, too—drop off a package, pick up some money, act as a lookout on other jobs."

"There was illegality?"

"They're satanists. Values are inverted. But so is the boy's life, for a while. It's a great feeling to be accepted and have everything you want after a lifetime of isolation. And without guilt. He's secure in the cell; it's his new family. He has less to do with his old life and even his schoolwork is neglected. His grades fall terribly."

"It meant nothing to him, I suppose."

"He's happy, yes. But then he isn't. Once again, the limitations of language. How can you express—in the great way it deserves—the titanic conflict of a young man's yearnings? Not just any young man, but a boy who's been tossed about by extremists with their own agendas. His success in life means nothing to them. He's clay to be formed to their own selfish ends, their perversions."

"You mean the satanists?"

"*All* the satanists, by whatever names."

He lapsed into brooding, the air seeming heavy in the darkening apartment. Dysmas soon left, knowing the story must wait until the problem of language was resolved. Maybe his sister helped him with this, loyally visiting and offering encouragement. She didn't show for a while, though, and Robert was increasingly self-absorbed. His high-class friends stopped coming. He even forgot his rent payment, though he suddenly remembered and came hanging on Dysmas's door.

"Hold on!" Dysmas called. "I was in the tub!"

"Oh, I'm sorry! I just remembered the rent and—"

"That's all right. Just let me get my robe on."

"I'll come back later. Or why don't you just come visit?"

"Well, sure. But you can leave the rent, if you want."

A check slid under the door.

"I still want you to visit," said Robert. "I've done some more of the poem. Come for tea, will you?"

Dysmas agreed to. Robert was quickly gone, Dysmas listening to his athletic descent. It occurred to him that Robert seemed perfect, a prototype of youth, yet within him something was eating away. Nothing physical like cancer, but something that eroded the spirit of his creativity. In hearing about the poem, Dysmas thought, he might learn what was going on.

"The cell wants more and more from him," Robert related.

"The satanists?"

"Yes. Stealing, sex without dignity, and they won't let him drift away. They've got those videotapes on him. They'll send them to his parents, the school. And his parents think he's crazy, take him to a deprogrammer. The boy doesn't cooperate—can't really, since the last counselor he had made a pass at him."

"He was stuck, then."

"Yes. But of course there's his godmother, and the postman. It's desperation more than anything, but it makes him go along with them, with whatever they want just so it'll wipe out the shame, the pressure—"

"They saved him from suicide, maybe?"

Robert stared at Dysmas, confused.

"Suicide? What's that? We do it with every move we make, only it doesn't always work. No, it's more than that. They provide him with revenge, a planned attack on the cell. The postman and his friends do some shooting, set a fire, make it look like a ritual. Everyone thinks the cell destroyed itself so the boy and his avengers are free. They're free to wallow in more advanced satanism, a world of drugs and trashy music and magazines, videos worse than the cell's, and always guns, loud vehicles, more guns. A taste for the degenerate, the sexual and sadistic."

"His godmother?"

"The postman, mostly. But she's the boy's link to him. She has a weakness for mass culture, the worst of it."

"And this grated on the boy, of course. He was sensitive, a reader of classics, one who'd developed a taste for beauty, refinement."

Robert stared again, a flicker of resentment passing. Resentment at being known, Dysmas thought.

"He has nowhere else to go," Robert said. "Not yet an adult, he has to endure. But as he becomes an adult, they want him to join their groups—occult, secretive, violent toward enemies. He goes with the postman to a meeting in timber country. Everyone's showing their guns, sharing hatreds. They talk about a radio host who's been knocking them. A month later, the man is dead."

"They planned it there?"

Robert said nothing.

"But surely, the boy wasn't in on it. Right?"

"That doesn't matter," Robert said. "The point is—the constant, killing point—you're always being tested. Tested so you can be used. If one gang doesn't get you the next one will, hounding you till you join them, stay with them. Life on the level of pit bulls, trained to be vicious. That's what they offer, anyway, what they stand for."

"Of course, we can rise above all that."

Robert looked irritated.

"Yes, rise above. Do a song and dance to please another gang."

"No, I meant live a separate life—cultivate beauty and grace, taste. As you do, Robert."

Dysmas thought this would comfort the young man, assure him. But Robert left his seat and went to the windows, pushing aside the curtain of hanging plants. He stood with hands in pockets, staring fixedly into a murky evening. He wanted to be alone now, Dysmas thought.

The sister returned quite suddenly, appearing at Dysmas's door a few evenings later. Her brother wasn't home, she said, and she had to get a message to him—his godmother was dying! The pale young woman seemed earnest, so Dysmas checked his card file for Robert's phone number at work. He made the call himself and was answered by a gruff male voice. Robert couldn't come to the phone, he was told, and no, they didn't take messages.

"I'll have to go there," he told the sister.

"Should I go with you?"

She didn't really want to, Dysmas thought. She was just sensing obligation.

"That's okay. I'll open his apartment and you can wait there, if you want."

"I should be getting back, though."

"All right, don't worry. I'll take care of it."

He shared her concern, perhaps exceeded it. So it was fitting he should go, add one more to the layers of guilt that consumed Robert. The news might be easier to hear from himself, and Robert wouldn't be pressed to respond.

The address, as it turned out, was a theater of sorts. Drinks were served in abundance and there was buffet supper. On a stage, distant from the entrance, people were singing and playing instruments. Dysmas stood watching until his view was blocked by a tall man in black suit.

"No free samples, sir. It's twenty dollars cover for the night."

"I'm looking for Robert Duggan. I understand he works here."

"Twenty bucks cover."

"I called a little earlier. I have an important message for him. See, his sister—"

"Hey, Stuka!" the suited man called.

A larger man with low brows made his way through the customers.

"Throw out this deadbeat."

"No, wait!" Dysmas blurted. "I've got the cover."

He wasn't sure he did but, on checking his wallet, found that he had enough. The surly greeter, checked in his wielding of authority, took the money resentfully.

"Enjoy yourself," he muttered.

Dysmas drifted edgily among the customers, who were mostly male and raucous. The entertainment matched the crowd, consisting of loud, raunchy songs by singers in flashy, revealing dresses. The stage was without props and the costumes tasteless, so Dysmas wondered what Robert might do here that was free-lance creative. At a break in the act he saw Stuka, the bouncer, approach one of the singers. The singer wore a purple and silver dress, brief on all sides to display a lithe, sensual body beneath. She had long, tumbling brown curls and was well bronzed. Except she wasn't a she, Dysmas suddenly realized. Stuka was pointing at him and Robert was looking back, suddenly shedding his assumed femininity. The other singers, Dysmas noticed, were also falsely female."

"You have to call me Chica here," were Robert's first words.

He seemed irritated, though not really embarrassed. But then, he was dressed correctly as far as most here were concerned.

"I won't call you anything," Dysmas said. "I'll just tell you what your sister told me: Your godmother's dying. Whatever passed between you in the past, somebody thought it important that you know. That's the only reason I came here. Your protector there doesn't take phone calls, and he charged me twenty dollars to stand here with you."

Robert looked away, yielding a side view of harsh makeup. Dysmas saw that the moustache he'd worn was fake.

"I have to get back," Robert said. "I'll get the twenty to you tomorrow."

He hesitated, staring at the mirror behind the bar. In the seconds that passed his eyes showed fear, but it exited with a head shake.

"Need any help?" Dysmas asked.

"No, it's all right. I'll be taking off early. Thanks for the message."

He turned away and strode to the stage, slowing on the way to assume his feminine gait.

Dysmas left, convinced he should not have come. But then, he thought later, if the woman had died while Robert was performing, the delay of message might well have been resented. As it was, he had done his best. He'd rewarded Robert's confidence by bringing him the news.

When he returned from his godmother's funeral, Robert was diffident toward Dysmas. He did resume his friendships with high-class people, well dressed and mannered like himself. Perhaps this protected him from discussing his poem, his epic. Dysmas was curious about it but guessed it would end unhappily. He left Robert to the fashionable ones, only watching from a distance. He preferred to think of Robert as the furniture stripper, bronze and gleaming as he toiled under the falling sun.

⚊⚬⚊

Dysmas had seemed upbeat and optimistic on his move to building manager, but as time wore on there were signs of shaky performance. Delayed payments of rent increased, three or four tenants continual deadbeats, with one who was effectively a squatter. Complaints about the building or the janitor came directly to our office instead of being screened by Dysmas. He was apparently focused on getting along with people—personal relationships—rather than standing firm on business matters.

"I don't think we can stick with him much longer," Sheila said to me, "not the way he's going. The CFO will be doing his review of properties soon. That building stands out like a white elephant."

We were in her apartment, snowflakes whipping about the windows, bread baking fragrantly in the oven. It was Saturday.

"Sorry it's turning out this way," I said.

"Well, I guess it was my idea. I'd cover for him if I could, but I don't see how I can. Hate it happening to a lifelong friend of yours."

"Yes. Thing is, though, he seems to have a problem with judgment, with decisions. To confront or not confront, to connect with someone or not connect, and so on. He's got something deep inside that exerts a force on him, thwarts his efforts."

"Does he have some place to go after—well, I mean, when he needs to move on?"

We were having herbal tea, the flavor Egyptian licorice. I inhaled its steam while sipping reflectively.

"Actually, he has this brother-in-law, one of several. They saw each other over the holidays at a get-together. This in-law has a business out in the boondocks, Pete's Perennials, inherited from his father and then expanded. This Pete is quite ambitious, and both he and Dysmas's sister are social climbers, wannabe at least. Anyway, Pete has been cozying up to a society artist who's been contracted by the city to beautify the parkways between downtown and the lake. He beat out other bidders for the subcontract by offering materials and labor for nothing except some of the artist's works. It'll be a financial loss for Pete but he wants the publicity and, truth be told, a foothold among the elite set."

"So how exactly does this affect Dysmas?"

"Well, coming into the city to monitor his workers will be taking Pete away from his perennial farm, so he needs someone to manage the place in his absence. There's a skeleton crew that will have to be watched, deliveries and such, and the family home is on the property. They're used to having Pete around during the day, so he thinks having Lucy's brother there will make her and the children feel more secure."

"So that's the job? Manage someone's business while guarding their family? Dysmas?"

"I know it invites skepticism. But it might not be all that daunting. Dysmas says Pete just wants him around the place, a person he can trust because he's family. That and because he's a manager already, sort of."

"Yeah, 'sort of.'"

"It's just the title that's operative."

"Well, not for the firm much longer. If that's the best he can do, or all he's got, you should tell him to take the plunge, Mac. Help him see the writing on the wall."

She got up to check the bread in the oven. We returned to our normal Saturday afternoon, the latest Dysmas issue perhaps resolved. Privately, I wondered how and when my involvement with him might end, assuming such was possible short of death.

6.

There was not, at first, much for Dysmas to do as assistant manager of Pete's Perennials. The eponymous owner seemed to have things well in hand, ably supported by his foreman, Rodrigo, who relayed Pete's instructions to the Spanish-speaking workers. Loads of rich earth and mulch arrived, along with plant food, special nutrients, and containers for transport. Dysmas mostly observed or sat by the phone in the battered shack that served as office and lunchroom. As the weather warmed, however, Pete began commuting to the site of the project to confer and plan with the society artist and park officials. Dysmas was obliged to make regular rounds through the fields and confer with Rodrigo about progress with the plants, which were mostly wildflowers to fulfill the vision of the artist. He felt somewhat bogus in this role, but the plants were soon ready for transport to the site. There was great activity for a time with the digging up and loading on trucks, then a sudden calmness as Pete, Rodrigo, and most of the workers were gone for the planting. It was a laborious process, much effort and care required, while Dysmas was left back at the farm with a few women, an elderly man, and a boy.

"Guess he didn't leave you much to work with," Lucy said.

"Oh, they're all right," Dysmas responded. "The ladies get on old Hector a bit, but he takes it in stride."

They were having lunch in the house, a good distance from the office-lunchroom shack. Dysmas felt grateful for this break in his day. His sister was a familiar comfort.

"There's the very young ones," she resumed. "The boy and the one girl a little older. I suppose they should be in school."

Dysmas just grunted. He was loath to criticize Pete's hiring or anything else about the situation. This was a haven for him.

"Oh, well," Lucy went on. "The school year is almost over. Soon our own kids will be around, too."

"Do they get involved in the business?" Dysmas inquired.

"The business?" His sister looked surprised. "No, there's the camps. Quite a variety now for the different skills and sports."

Dysmas felt slightly abashed. He should have realized, he thought, that after their home environment in childhood, the harshness, Lucy would strive to be liberal toward her children.

"That's fine," he said to her. "Hope they have a great time."

He didn't mind making his rounds through the fields now since so few workers were around. He noticed then that the boy and girl of whom Lucy had spoken were often working together, the age factor engendering closeness. Neither of them spoke English. The girl, Lupita, spoke Spanish like most of the workers while the boy, Leonid, spoke only with his mother in a Slavic language. As the days passed, Dysmas observed Lupita apparently teaching Spanish expressions to Leonid, who was receptive and became confident with her. The former monk became fascinated with the process, sensed that it held some special meaning for him that he couldn't quite decipher. He reflected on it during long evenings in the mobile home Pete had leased for him.

During one of his lunchtime visits to the house, another guest arrived to join Dysmas and his sister for the meal. Lucy introduced her as Vera, a fellow member of their church's bible study group. She was tall for a woman and wore no makeup. Dysmas felt an affinity toward her though he was sure they'd never met before. When the conversation turned to Lucy's children and their doings, Dysmas was inspired to mention Lupita and Leonid, their situation and adjustment to each other. Vera's interest was peaked.

"Do you become engaged with them?" she asked.

"Well, no. I'm there to supervise their work, them and the others. I give them plenty of leeway, though."

"Oh, yes. That's good of you. And have you had children yourself? Your own children?"

Dysmas was taken aback. He'd anticipated a child labor question. "No," he responded.

"Dysmas has been a monk," Lucy said in explanation.

"Oh, a monk!" Vera's expression was one of wonder.

"Yes," Dysmas acknowledged, inwardly cringing.

"Then you must know a lot about the Focolare Movement."

Actually, he knew almost nothing. They were just one of countless church groups to him. His time in the monastery was consumed by fulfilling his emotional needs.

"Vera is a member," Lucy further revealed.

"That's great," Dysmas nodded. "Yeah, really great."

Unwilling or unable to discuss his monastic life, he waited for the conversation to abandon religion. He left to return to work at the first opportunity. When Pete later learned about the luncheon from Lucy, he brought it up with Dysmas at the shack.

"You know," he confided, "they take vows, those Focolare."

"Vows? Just to be in the group?"

"The actual members, sure. Poverty, obedience, and *chastity.*"

"But it's not a religious order."

"They do it anyway. I don't know, maybe they're wannabes, came along too late. Or else rejects for some reason."

"So, all their income goes to the organization, there's someone they have to obey without question, and—" Dysmas hesitated.

"You got it, brother. No sexual intercourse—ever, at all, for any reason."

It was a friendly warning, Dysmas perceived, Pete wanting to caution him against a dubious involvement, protecting him as a relative. He meant well, and alerts against poverty and blind obedience were well taken, but to warn Dysmas about required abstinence was a masterpiece of irony, albeit unintended.

"Wow," the former monk responded, "that's really something."

Vera, in his thinking, went from an acquaintance of no importance to a fascinating personage, a pleasant obsession. The idea of a like-minded or asexual woman seemed to offer a solution to him, freedom from the recurring fear of abnormality and its discovery by others. On researching Vera's organization, he found that Focolare sought to imitate the mother of Christ in their lives. This wasn't as important to Dysmas as it once would have been, but it sealed his mental image of Vera. Though not especially attractive and somewhat ungainly, she was close enough to his ideal to occupy his thoughts in the flower fields.

There was a problem with accessibility, though. She was not a statue in the woods. He might see her at lunch some more, but Lucy and soon Pete would be there. There would also be others at her church services and, of course, the bible study group. At home, she lived with roommates to economize the Focolare way. That left her workplace, a regional hospital where she was a registered nurse. He would have to find a way to approach her there, Dysmas thought.

But before he was ready to act on this decision, events took a turn with the completion of Pete's project. A celebratory luncheon was held, nominally hosted by the city's mayor, who sat between the celebrity artist and the city parks director at the V.I.P. table. There were several dozen large round tables before the dais, mostly occupied by socialites and political types. At the very back and next to a fire exit were two seats reserved for Pete and his assistant, Dysmas getting the nod over Rodrigo. Pete at first questioned their seat assignments, requiring the maître d' to consult his paperwork. They were found to be correct, to Pete's consternation, so he and Dysmas settled in with two giggling secretaries and somebody's chauffeur. Several chairs were vacant. The table next to theirs, slightly more central, was used by three city policemen smoking their complementary cigars.

Pete was unable, after the speechmaking and meal, to approach the celebrity artist, who accompanied the mayor on his exit behind a phalanx of guards and stooges. Pete still had some notes in his suitcoat for a short talk he'd wanted to give up on the dais. These were now stuffed with some force into a trash bin as he and Dysmas passed it. The drive back to the farm was accomplished in silence, Pete bristling behind the wheel and Dysmas letting him stew. He'd had his fill of hearing angry complaints while managing the apartment building.

The next day, after staying at the house all morning, Pete had Dysmas and Rodrigo sign as witnesses to a letter he was sending the artist by certified mail. It was essentially a demand for the portion of the artist's work that Pete had been promised in return for materials and labor on the beautificátion project. No mention was made of the banquet snubbing, but the letter's tone would no doubt bring it to mind. Pete left for the nearest post office to get the letter off immediately, then repaired to the house on his return. Dysmas was left to manage the full crew and operations for virtually the entire day.

Pete returned in good spirits the next morning, brushing aside Dysmas's worry about his management the day before, possible errors in the unexpected role.

"It'll all come out in the wash," Pete laughed. "Important thing is we got that letter off. It's all about priorities. Principles take priority!"

He nodded for emphasis, tight-lipped, as he surveyed his land.

"I tried to call him first. Has all his calls now going to a publicist. Just doing interview requests and endorsements, she said. No guarantee he'd call back."

"Why do you think he's acting this way?" Dysmas asked.

"Swelled head. They get their fifteen minutes and they think they're glowing gods."

It appeared Pete had dealt with the slight decisively, at least to his own satisfaction, so his business could again function normally. Work on the farm had fallen behind during the project, a backlog of orders awaiting fulfillment, but with Pete and the additional workers around they would soon be caught up. Dysmas felt some relief with decreased responsibilities and more freedom to strategize for his approach to Vera. He was about to make a trip to her place of employment, dropping in around the end of her shift, when an unusual package arrived at Pete's Perennials.

"This here is marked *personal*," said Rodrigo in the office shack.

It was a long, wide, but rather flat brown carton, not especially heavy. Dysmas glanced et the return address, thought a moment, let an idea register.

"Better go get Pete," he told the foreman.

When their boss came in, he lifted the carton and studied the address label. He raised his eyebrows and nodded noncommittally.

"It's from him," Pete said.

He borrowed Rodrigo's knife and carefully slit the tapes on the box. Packing peanuts trickled out as he raised the flaps, revealing more such peanuts that he swept away. There was a small painting inside, about twelve by ten inches, and another the same size beneath it. The first pictured a few pieces of fruit in a bowl, the second a single flower in a long-necked vase. The frames were plain unfinished slats. A photocopy of Pete's letter to the artist lay between the paintings, *Paid in Full* printed across it in red ink. Pete stared at the sheet a moment, then laid it aside and picked up the paintings, one in each hand, and displayed them to Rodrigo.

"What do you think, Rod?"

The foreman shrugged, spreading his hands.

"Don't know much about art, Pete."

"Dysmas, how about you?"

The assistant was given a direct view. Both works were unpleasing in aspect, the first looking mildewed along an edge, the second uneven in coloration, perhaps faded.

"Okay, I guess."

Pete laid the paintings back in their box, closed the flaps and pushed it aside. He picked up the ersatz packing slip and appeared to study it, then laid it deliberately in the middle of his desk. Returning to the box, he picked it up and held it out toward Dysmas.

"Do me a favor, will you? Take this down to the house and leave it with Lucy. Stay with her awhile." Then, to Rodrigo: "We're closing for the day. Send the workers home, tell them to come back tomorrow."

——•——

Dysmas had experienced doubts about his plan to visit Vera at her workplace. She might not be able to get away if he showed up during her shift, or she might have things to do right at quitting time. He might be better off calling to make an appointment, he'd thought, though then he'd run the risk of rejection over the phone. Now there was this new situation, perhaps an opportunity, with Pete closing the business for half a day. It opened a window of time through which

Dysmas could operate calmly and precisely in his approach, lying in wait if necessary. He'd already called the personnel office at the hospital, ostensibly seeking employment, so he had his driving directions and knew the hours of the shifts.

Cruising the hospital's parking areas, he thought he saw Vera's car, a small red sedan, in a section reserved for staff. He parked the old pickup he was using, courtesy of Pete, within sight of the car and Vera's likely exit. It occurred to Dysmas that he shouldn't follow her through traffic since that could be construed as stalking. In addition, once she reached her residence there'd be the roommates to consider. He'd have to catch her on foot before she drove away.

He got out of the truck and loitered by it as if waiting to give someone a ride. Vera soon came out in conversation with another nurse, waving good-bye as they parted. Dysmas strode forward.

"Hello, Vera."

She halted in mid-motion, car keys in hand. It took a few seconds for her to recognize him.

"Hello."

"How are you today?"

"Just getting off. Are you a patient here?"

He was tempted to lie and say he was. But the inspiration was too sudden, not thought out.

"No, I came to see you. Talk with you."

She didn't respond, smiled uncomprehendingly.

"Can we go somewhere?" he asked. "To talk?"

"Well, there's a little coffee shop inside, just off the lobby."

"Fine."

The coffee place was hardly separate from the lobby proper, people walking by on their medical business close to the tables. Like talking with her in a shopping mall, Dysmas thought. Vera seemed to notice his discomfort.

"There's also the chapel," she said, perhaps hopefully.

"No, this is okay."

They bought two cups of coffee with Vera's employee card and sat uneasily at one of the tiny tables. Dysmas sensed Vera's burgeoning religiosity, also the debasement of his own. He suddenly didn't know where to start in this meeting that he'd so looked forward to.

"Do you have much contact with your order?" she asked. "*Former* order?"

He thought a moment before answering.

"No. They're a rather obscure group. Not much contact with the outside world."

He needed to say more, he thought, direct the conversation. Then he remembered from somewhere: when in doubt, ask questions. Ask questions about the other.

"What about you? Do you have much contact with the Focolare order?"

Vera looked surprised, but pleasantly. She smiled and composed herself, gazing into the middle distance.

"Well, it's more a movement than an order. As such, it's all over the world. By my way of life, the movement's way, I'm in constant contact with it and its patron, the Virgin Mary."

Her mention of a way of life alerted Dysmas, brought his purpose back into focus.

"This way of living you have, that Focolare teaches, I've heard it involves taking vows like in a usual religious order."

Vera looked serious.

"Yes, there are vows taken. It's required to become a member. We also have a great many supporters, non-members, who don't take the vows."

"Which are?"

"Obedience, poverty, chastity."

She lowered her voice in speaking the third, unlike Pete who'd emphasized it.

"Those must be difficult at times for the members."

"It varies from person to person. One gets used to them after a time, sees their value. But you took them yourself, didn't you? In your order?"

"That was different. A closed environment so easily enforced. Spiritual support." They called it, he almost added. "But your members are out in the world, on your own. Self-enforcement only."

"I don't think of it quite that way."

"No, of course not. But suppose you met someone who respected your vows and would never interfere with your keeping them, but in all other ways could serve as—well, a 'significant other.' A special support for you, as you would be for him."

A flicker of alarm crossed Vera's face at the word *him*.

"Well, I have my roommates, the Church, the movement, Bible study, my coworkers—"

"Aren't there married couples within the Focolare?" Dysmas interrupted.

"Yes, of course. But they're all supporters as far as I know, not members. The chastity vow, obviously, would preclude—"

"What if the man is by nature not drawn to women sexually? Or to anyone at all?"

Vera was visibly bothered. Dysmas knew that he'd gone too far, too fast, but he'd felt a need to fully explain himself, still felt it.

"I don't know what to say," Vera faltered.

"Good," Dysmas blurted inexplicably.

"Good?"

"Yes, because I want you as my perfect woman and I've had to tell you that. Your silence allows me to tell you."

Vera tried to force a smile.

"Are you feeling all right, Dysmas? Are you joking?"

"No. I'm all right and I'm not joking. I'm perfectly sincere. Believe me."

She looked around at people in the vicinity, began to cry.

"Accept my love," Dysmas persisted. "The mystery of my love."

Vera raised a hand toward someone in the distance, wiped her tears with a napkin.

A security guard, sighting one of the nurses in distress, approached their table. His partner held back but watched intently.

———◦———

Advancing through the flower fields, Dysmas approached the point where Lupita and Leonid were working. Pete had gone into the city to see his lawyer about the paintings, leaving his assistant in charge, while Rodrigo was occupied with a mechanic who serviced the farm's vehicles and other equipment. The two children were working assiduously as if they'd seen Dysmas patrolling. Usually, he knew, they engaged in frequent chatter hindered only by a limited common vocabulary, which nonetheless seemed to be growing. Leonid was on his way to becoming a bilingual worker who did not speak English. A cheap course at the library or community college could make him trilingual, a credential for working that might compensate for his poor education.

"Good work!" Dysmas called out, receiving two sunny smiles in return.

He moved on. If it were just that easy, he thought, picturing again his rejection and then ejection from the hospital. Somehow things always fell apart, despite his making what he considered his best and most promising effort. He might have been lazy on occasion, sometimes impulsive, but these were common traits that many people had and yet they still succeeded. Why did he get no slack in life? Not that he suspected a conspiracy against him. He was above that, of course. But what was wrong with people? With the world? He wasn't out to do harm, after all, or to strike back. Maybe he should be, but he wasn't. No, he *definitely* wasn't.

Returning to the shack, he heard Rodrigo and the mechanic arguing in Spanish in the lunchroom. It seemed a friendly enough argument, the mechanic, whose name was Calixto, pressing his contention while Rodrigo offered brief retorts. Dysmas delayed making his presence known, still mired in his self-centered jumble of thoughts. When the other men came through the office to exit, Calixto suddenly halted and stared at Dysmas at his desk.

"No habla español," Rodrigo said to his friend. "Adelante, me iré enseguida."

The foreman directed the mechanic towards the door. Calixto left. Rodrigo watched him go, then resignedly turned to Dysmas.

"He is a little upset."

"Oh? Why is that?"

"Well, that guy stiffing Pete. Now this lawsuit about it. Could be much trouble for people."

"For Calixto?"

"Not just him. All the workers. You, too. Pete's family even. That lawyer Pete uses, very expensive. Already a big loss from doing that artist work. Rich guy like that drags out the hearings, hopes the other side gives up. Pete always gave us bonuses for the fall slowdown, then Christmas. None of that now. Lucky to get our regular pay."

"Maybe Pete can win the lawsuit."

"Win what? More paintings? Even if Pete sold them, it would be for peanuts. You saw the ones that came. That guy is no good artist. He just fools people."

"I don't know what to say, Rodrigo. It does sound bad."

"Maybe you can talk to him. You're family. Make him see this is a bad move. He should pull back, sooner the better."

Dysmas imagined himself trying to counsel Pete, a man of such vigor, pride, and professional heritage. The absurdity of it almost made him laugh.

"I'm sure we'll be talking about it," he said. "I'll try to work that in, that option."

Dysmas for once had no illusions about something. He had no intention of trying to stop Pete, throwing humane reasoning against prodigious pride, but he thought there might be another angle, something beyond Rodrigo's view, that could turn the lawsuit into something more than a boondoggle. That very pride of Pete's, its injury by the artist's callousness, the resulting effects on Pete's functioning in his business and his family, might be key to a greater claim for damages than insufficient artwork. The expensive lawyer should be able to do something with the idea, Dysmas thought, but he needed to be discreet, run it by someone he trusted before presenting it to Pete.

He decided to call me. We hadn't spoken in some time, both of us preoccupied with events in our private lives. It was a weekday evening.

"Is Sheila there with you?" he asked.

"No, she isn't. Actually, we decided we'd both play the field for a while. She met this lawyer at a business seminar."

"Oh. Yeah, I just asked since this is kind of confidential."

"No problem. So what's going on with you, Dys?"

He gave me a rundown on events at the farm and the city project, mentioned a relationship of sorts that he'd explain later. When he got to the crisis inspiring his call, he sounded enthusiastic about his imagined plan for a solution.

"What do you think, Mac? Should I present it to Pete? Just sort of float it like an idea from a relative?"

"Well, you're also assistant manager. You'd bear some responsibility for the result, with some people anyway. Like your sister."

"Okay, fine. But what about the action? Is it feasible?"

I had to think, set aside what I knew about Dysmas and his past, consider only this specific set of facts and the degree of logic in what was proposed.

"Was there a contract between Pete and this artist?" I asked to clarify.

"No, just between the artist and the city."

"So, Pete and the rest of you were working under a handshake deal, for just some paintings."

"Yeah. Though I don't know if they shook hands."

The inanity of the activities and the thinking behind them overwhelmed me. Dysmas's plan would be a second layer of mushy thinking on top of Pete's. My friend's involvement with the farm, which he seemed eager to extend, was exquisitely deflating.

"Listen, Dysmas. I think you need to get out of there, quit Pete's Perennials as soon as possible."

"What! Why?"

"Without a written contract, with all pertinent details and signed and preferably witnessed, Pete is not going to get a favorable judgment. It sounds like he didn't even specify which paintings he expected to get, or at least the number, and what the extent of his work would be. Agreeing to bear the expense of all materials and labor was, well, just crazy."

Dysmas was silent, perhaps shocked.

"Hello? Are you there, Dys?"

"Yeah, I'm here. I get you, Mac, but why do I have to leave the farm? I've been doing okay here, mostly."

"It's taking a huge financial hit, Dys. He might even ask you to work with no salary for a while, as family. You can't afford that. It's the wrong direction for you in life. Pack your stuff and get out. You can stay with me awhile until you get something else."

"What about Lucy? She's my sister."

"And Pete's wife. That's a contract that sticks. She was there long before you arrived. They'll be needing each other to get through this. As they will, I think, and they'll have learned from the experience."

There was a pause before Dysmas spoke again.

"Can I get back to you on this? It seems awful sudden, just throwing everything over. I need to think it all through."

"Of course, Dys."

But he was still thinking things over when, a few days after our conversation, there was a "breaking news" story on television that the celebrity artist had been murdered. It had happened in his luxury condo, where a large blood-stained wrench was found near the body. Police had no one in custody but were fanning out to interview the victim's known associates, who were many.

Dysmas soon arrived at my door, duffel bag in tow.

7.

In doing his research on the Focolare, Dysmas had run across an article on the Enneagram, a geometric figure resembling a nine-pointed star with its points connected by a circle. Each point is connected by straight lines to two other points on the circle, thus forming the star-like figure. To believers in The Enneagram of Personality, the nine points represent interconnected personality types. Each of them has negative behaviors that can be converted to positive ones by the personality type at the end of one connecting line. The other connecting line is to a type that can *be* improved by the type at the first point.

The article was written by one of two Charismatic Catholic priests who'd taken a course on the Enneagram at a Jesuit university. While the author did not pursue the subject further, his companion was deeply swayed and left his ministry to promote it. He cofounded a self-improvement center in rural Minnesota catering to both business clients and troubled individuals. The center offered seminars, short retreats, and longer-term treatment. The ex-priest's partner was a female psychiatrist with whom he resided.

Dysmas had dismissed the article during his approach to Vera and the crisis at the farm, but his interest was renewed with his move to my apartment. With no other template for his future, he wondered which of the nine points on the Enneagram represented his own personality, with another point connected that could refine his negative traits into unimagined strengths. The article went only so far, not getting into the process for transformation, and Dysmas concluded that physical presence in a formal program would be necessary if he were to benefit. The center in Minnesota headed by an ex-priest and a psychiatrist seemed a promising resource for him in his quest.

"Are you sure you want to get into this?" I asked him. "You don't need to rush into anything. You've got management experience now. Shouldn't take long to land a decent job."

"No, I need to change myself, Mac. Going job-to-job hasn't worked for me. This program will let me change myself and that will change what happens to me. I don't know how, exactly, but if it works for other people then it's going to work for me."

My reluctance to discourage him muzzled my skepticism of the Enneagram movement. It was to me just a mishmash of notions, vague and without factual or logical basis. Its own adherents had often disagreed and revised its teachings. It had even been dismissed as pseudoscience by real professionals after careful analysis. But it had occasionally been popular since its inception in the 19th century, so Dysmas was just one in a suggestible legion that had been drawn by its allure.

"Well," I said resignedly, "just remember: If my guest room by chance is not available, there's always a spot for you on my floor."

———◆———

The bus stopped for Dysmas across the road from what appeared to be a closed motel. There was no identifying sign but it appeared well-kept, albeit simple and unadorned. Some distance behind the old motel, to one side and upon a hillock, stood an imposing house. It was accessible by a cinder drive that branched off the road. A sign with arrow directed visitors down the drive to the Center for Enlightened Culture.

Advancing up the drive, Dysmas noticed a number of yurts erected on another hillock across some cultivated land. There was no activity around them, nor in the intervening fields. There were no other structures in sight except a shed behind the great house. Encroaching forest and the uneven landscape limited one's view, concealing the small lakes and meadows for which the area was noted. The crops Dysmas saw were various and disorganized, much of the land furrowed but unplanted, giving the impression of an urban community garden transplanted en masse. Reaching the house, he saw it was in remarkably good condition for one of Victorian design. A minivan with *C.E.C.* on it was parked in front, along with a small sedan. He rang the house's doorbell but, receiving no response, was obliged to bang with a heavy knocker decorated with a scowling face.

A mild-looking man with crewcut and rimless glasses peeked through an opening.

"May I help you?"

"I'm Brother Dysmas. I talked on the phone with Prue the other day."

"Talked on the phone? About coming here?"

"Yes. Didn't she tell you?"

A hesitation, then: "Oh, yes. Come in, Brother. I'm Edgar."

He was led into spacious rooms decorated with oriental rugs and furniture of about the same vintage as the house. The artwork on the walls, however, was mostly abstract with a large enneagram symbol fashioned from rattan in front of the main window. Dysmas observed its dominant shadow as he settled himself in a creaking chair, finally releasing the small suitcase I'd exchanged with him for his duffel bag.

"I'll go and find Prue," said the ex-priest.

He was gone about ten minutes, during which time a young woman in apron passed through the room, glanced indifferently at Dysmas, and continued on. Edgar returned with a rather pale woman with wild dark hair streaked with gray. She gave a toothy smile and sat on one end of a couch, holding a shawl about her shoulders. Edgar sat alertly next to her.

"Welcome to the Center," Prue said, "and the beginning of your journey."

"Journey?"

"Your journey to enlightenment." Then, when Dysmas didn't respond: "So, tell us about yourself—where you've been, what you've done, what you wish to transform."

He launched into a sketchy account of his life, omitting the earliest years. Prue's face registered a variety of emotions as she heard him out—frowning, smiling, eyebrows raised, jaw dropping in astonishment. Twice she emitted a shrieking laugh, unnerving with the prominent teeth.

"So," she said as he finished, "that has been the path that brought you here. That was its value, of course, you can see that." She paused as if reflecting. "You know, Dysmas, I'd like to speak with Edgar briefly in another room. Can you wait here a few minutes?"

"Yes, of course."

"Of course," she smiled, and they got up and left.

While they were gone, the young woman in apron returned and this time hesitated near Dysmas.

"You'll be taken in, then?" she asked in a British accent.

"I think so," he answered.

"Will you be in the barrack or the huts?"

"I don't know. They're discussing."

She continued through without speaking further. When the cofounders returned, Prue appeared pleased and Edgar resolute. They resumed their seats.

"On listening to your story," Prue began, "we think you're somewhat advanced from our usual retreaters. Your experience, with its variety, its intensity, has well prepared you for the adjustments to your personality, for inner and outer transformation. We'd like to offer you an enhanced version of the therapeutic experience, one that will bring you to the level of a staff member here at the Center. Which, potentially, you may become if you choose."

"We're somewhat short of our model faculty just now," Edgar added. "Our ideal operation calls for five resident mentors, but we're down to just the two of us and one on extended leave."

"Seniya," said Prue. "A truly sublime young woman. I do so miss her."

"Financially speaking," Edgar went on, "the resident mentors share equally in the funds we take in, after expenses of course."

"Would I be staying in the barrack?" Dysmas asked. "Or one of the yurts?"

"God, no!" Prue reacted. "I'll have Diamond refresh a gable for you. The work residence and meditation huts we use for clients."

"We sometimes get groups, companies," Edgar added. "The companies are always in the barrack, their work residence. Right now, there's just a couple of singles in the huts."

"You can wait in the library while she gets the gable ready," said Prue. "The library is up on the second level, north side. There's material on the Enneagram there you can use to get oriented. Then you can rest a bit and we'll see you at dinner."

"Okay," Dysmas consented.

The library was about the size of a large bedroom with a single window looking out on a hazy northern sky. Up close, it revealed a dull rural landscape with a column of industrial smoke on the near horizon. One wall was mostly covered by shelves of psychological and psychiatric books, journals, magazines, and binders of loose materials. The opposite wall featured a lesser amount of religious and philosophical texts. A few of the titles Dysmas recognized from the monastery. These dealt with teachings of the Church and lives of the saints, but there were also works of secular and even agnostic natures, along with studies of the Far Eastern religions. In the middle of the room was a plain wooden table and two straight-backed chairs, the materials on the Enneagram in a neat stack for his perusal.

In examining the booklets and pamphlets, Dysmas saw that the lines between three of the points on the enneagram symbol formed an equilateral triangle. According to the materials, these points represented three "central" personality types, each within one of three groupings of three types each. The groupings were called the three "centers of intelligence." Dysmas found that the names given to the nine personality types varied among the writers. They sometimes contradicted each other and were redundant in their descriptions, even labelling two of the *basic* personality types "achiever" and "succeeder." The negative traits ascribed to the types, referred to as "addictions" or "temptations," were in fact inclinations that might be had by anyone, regardless of personality. There was frequent recourse to allegory, little stories akin to fables or fairy tales, in writers' attempts to support their ideas. The vagueness and flaws continued to mount until Dysmas began to feel mentally awash in a sea of gibberish.

He sat back heavily in the hard chair. Some people saw meaning in this, he considered, but some also saw meaning in speaking in tongues. Then there were the holy rollers, faith healing, and the insistence on miracles within his own faith. Here, where he sat between a wall of psychiatry and a wall of religious fervency, wading through cultish devotion to a geometric symbol, he might as well be an overgrown mushroom in Alice's wonderland.

"I'm not sure I got the gist of things," he confessed at dinner later.

Prue and Edgar exchanged looks. Dishes were being served by Diamond and a heavyset cook whom Prue had called Dahlia.

"Don't worry about it," said Prue. "Most of what we'd consider training is experiential. We'll be right there to help you do the practicum."

"The terminology and such you'll pick up incidentally," Edgar added.

Most of the meal was vegetarian. The small single meat dish was very lean, dark, and already in thin slices.

"Venison," Edgar informed. "Shot it myself near here."

The quantity seemed meager for three people, especially considering the large animal it came from. Dysmas took a modest portion and passed the plate toward Prue, who waved it off.

"This experiential training," he ventured, "what exactly does it consist of?"

Edgar deferred to Prue, who assumed a thoughtful mien.

"Well, we try to take advantage of our location here, the many venues for quiet reflection and communion with nature it affords. To begin with, maybe tomorrow Edgar could take you to one of our special spots, a hidden source of epiphany for many of our clients."

"Sounds good. You won't be coming yourself?"

"No. At least one mentor must be here to handle business that arises."

"The helpers you see are not accountable," said Edgar.

"No hunting this trip. We don't want to start you out with violence."

"Hunting isn't violence," her partner retorted. "It's part of nature itself."

Prue smiled at Dysmas.

"You see? Even we have our little spats. That's part of nature, too."

———◆———

They took the small van with logo on its sides, Edgar driving within posted limits through farmland and forest. He turned into a narrow lane that rose and crossed some higher hills. It wound a bit and they passed a ravine, then came to a second, larger one. Edgar parked in some weeds on the solid side of the road.

"It's a cave," he told Dysmas, "a special one to us at the Center. I clean up after the animals from time to time. They always try to eat the candles. Be careful going down here."

The cave was near the bottom, concealed by an overhang and a tangle of brush and debris. Edgar frowned as he studied it, as if something in the arrangement bothered him.

"Seems they've already returned," he said.

"The candle-nibblers?"

"Yes."

"How can you tell? It looks to be almost covered."

"Almost, yes. But years of branch-weaving produces a method, and this isn't mine."

Dysmas was reminded of the huge enneagram symbol in the Center's parlor window.

"Yes," he said, "I'm sure it must take some skill."

They cleared the opening and proceeded into the earth, Edgar going first with a camping lantern. Streaks of minerals glistened from the walls. They passed a few hollows, soon approaching a larger one with a glow from the cavern beyond.

"I'll kill the lantern," Edgar said. "We're almost there."

He hung back, allowing Dysmas first entry. Instinctively, the ex-monk felt reverence as he leaned into the glow, peered ahead, squinted to distinguish a large solid object.

"The Great Stone Ring," Edgar announced.

Resembling a primitive wheel, it rested on its edge beneath the strange shaft of light that penetrated the hillside. Around it were the red and blue votive candles, as yet unlit, and before it a bundle of dry pussywillow.

"Looks undisturbed," Dysmas commented. "Guess your animals changed their minds."

"Or else they weren't animals."

"Someone checking it out, then. Trying to cover up. But who?"

"Come on, I'll light the candles."

They entered and squatted before the Ring . For a while they just sat, filling space and breathing air. The cave seemed a shelter from chaos and banality.

"To come to this spot," said Edgar, "sit with others in candlelight before the Great Ring, is to end our supposed differences in class. Our brotherhood replaces the pretensions of inherited culture. Look in there, the void of the firmament."

He was gazing into the Great Stone Ring. It was actually only a few feet away.

"The infinite potentiality of nothingness, the space that can be filled with anything. Within that void are the unified opposites, of which we can choose one, but the other still exists, forever inherent in our choice. And it applies to all: an infinite variety of beings and non-beings."

Edgar glanced around the cavern, his eyes coming to rest on the shaft of light from outside. He looked up as if to trace its course to the remote opening.

"The Pact of Hollowness. Shall we recite it now? Let its truth inspire us?"

"I'm afraid I don't know it," said Dysmas, bemused.

"Of course. Just listen to me, concentrate on the words:

Gaze at it; there is nothing to see.
It is called the formless.
Heed it; there is nothing to hear.

It is called the soundless.
Grasp it; there is nothing to hold on to.
It is called the immaterial.
We cannot inquire into these three,
Hence, they interfuse into one.
It is the evasive.
Approach it; you cannot see its face.
Go after it; you cannot see its back.

And thus we renew the Pact of Hollowness, girding us once again against the world."

Dysmas tried to imitate Edgar in his gazing at the hole in reverence. As he did so, though, a smile surfaced on one side of his face, the side away from his companion. To quash it he spoke.

"I suppose that, as we go on, we might seem to be greater—more knowledge, achievements and such—but in reality we might be lesser for having less choices available, doors having closed and all, so less potential."

"It goes deeper than that," Edgar responded. "The very quality of—say, our knowledge, was superior in our youth to what it is now. Then it was undifferentiated, more encompassing, more in balance. Now it's specialized to apply in practical situations, cutting us off from knowledge of the larger universe, the truth beyond our private, suffocating routines."

Dysmas tried to imagine himself as being wiser in his younger years. If that were true, why had he made decisions that resulted now in his sitting in this cave staring at a hole in a stone?

"Some of this might be beyond me," he said.

"Nonsense," Edgar retorted. "The potential for transcendence lies dormant within you. It's simply a matter of fusing those hidden qualities with those that are already manifest. Using what you have to be the beautiful self you truly are!"

Dysmas stared at him. Edgar gestured toward the huge stone.

"In unity with the ultimate force of the universe!"

Dysmas smiled.

"Transcendence!" the ex-priest shouted.

The ex-monk offered his hand, the best thing he thought he could do. Edgar accepted it. They sat with clasped hands in the glow of the cavern, seen only by the eye of the stone amid the candles—the Great Stone Ring, seeing nothing so seeing all. The two men peered at it, as if sensing the origin of what they were, and perhaps what would follow for them.

———•◦•———

At dinner that evening, Edgar remained enlivened by their trip to the cave, extolling its spiritual stimuli, Dysmas contributing brief agreements. Prue seemed to sense the hollowness of his remarks, however, likely expecting him to show a greater reaction. She was subdued toward Edgar's enthusiasm, shifting the conversation toward business matters. An insurance staff was due to arrive soon for a weekend of rejuvenation. It might be good, she thought, to have breakup sessions, with Dysmas handling one of the smaller groups.

"I don't know if I'm ready for that," he weakly protested.

"You will be by then, don't worry. I'll be helping you."

Alone that night in his gable room, he reviewed the events of the day, at first dominated by Edgar's fanaticism and a need to show concurrence with him. This place had the makings of a personal haven, Dysmas thought, one he might accept as a venue to meet his needs for growth and fulfillment. But now there was this suggestion—no, requirement—posited by Prue that was a challenge he had to meet to stay here. He'd once wanted to be a priest, stand before a suggestible flock and shepherd them. Fine for then, but much had since happened and now he was damaged goods, the teaching talents of the potential priest in tatters. Were they even still there at some level to be salvaged for his own material purposes? He didn't know.

He got up late the next day, having missed the regular breakfast, but was pleased to find that Dahlia had kept coffee and oatmeal warm. The sky outside was overcast, the air humid, and he saw Prue at a distance working in the vegetable plots with the yurt dwellers, one male and one female. Edgar was not in evidence. Dysmas decided to have a morning walk, headed down the drive towards the closed motel. Coming to the road, he turned and walked along its shoulder in the direction the bus had taken after letting him off. He hadn't gone far when he came to an inviting opening in the forest, wide enough to afford entry and progress without brambles and brush. There was further widening after several turns and he found himself in a clearing with the ruins of a small building in its center. Roofless, it was constructed of small boulders connected with a dissolving mortar, the remaining walls less than half their original height. There were three flat slabs along the perimeter affording low seating. Dysmas entered and rested on one of them.

He could stay in this place, he reflected, enjoy a peaceful interlude in his life, put up with the muddled teachings as payment for his residence. He might have to actually promote them, but couldn't he just consider that a job like any other? He hadn't felt morally bound in the other work he'd done so it could simply not matter here. Except, of course, that he'd be deceiving Prue and Edgar. But they were deceived already by the Enneagram and their acceptance of it, a false god. There was also the possibility he might mislead someone with his instruction, some especially suggestible soul. He would have to be vigilant against this, weaken his statements, avoid true proselytizing. With care, Dysmas thought, he could make it work.

He remained in the stone enclosure for some time, relishing his solitude under a gray sky, departing only with the onset of a breeze-borne drizzle. Back at the house, he encountered Prue as she was coming from her shower. She looked refreshed. He told her of his session in the small ruin and her face lit with interest.

"That's good, very good. So you found peace there."

"It was relaxing, yes. Until the rain came."

"Another manifestation of peace. The matrix of inspiration. You were inspired?"

"Well, I felt good. Relaxed, like I say."

Prue's smile was unchanging.

"It will come."

Dysmas didn't know what she meant, instinctively kept silent.

"There's another special place you should see. I'll be the one to take you this time. We'll go there in the morning. Sleep early tonight."

He wasn't sure whether her directness was a professional tactic—psychiatrist talk—or just Prue's own nature. Either way, he thought, it was a badge of her authority in this place. He accordingly followed her directions and was well rested for their excursion. They took the small sedan, Prue driving, and headed through the fragrant early morning to Willowsong Lake. They came to an intersecting road at which Edgar had turned right, but Prue turned left instead. The land became more wooded and they passed a few cabins.

"They're locked except for the boathouse," Prue informed. "Shall we walk along the shore or do you feel like rowing?"

"I guess I'm due for the exercise."

He pulled out a boat and they set off across the lake. Since the morning was windless, the dipping of oars made the only ripples. The only movement beyond was the billowing funnel of smoke from a distant food processing plant. Rhythmically rowing, Dysmas watched Prue sitting placidly in the stern. She appeared thoughtful as she looked out toward the shore, stayed so as she spoke from recollection:

"That which is best is similar to the water.
Water profits ten thousand things and does not oppose them.
It is always at rest in humble places.
Therefore, for staying, we prefer a humble place.
For companions, we prefer the kindness.
For actions, we prefer the right time."

She smiled and he saw her as a child of nature, a flame from the fire of life, which overall never died.

"I like that," he said reflexively.

A banal comment, yet she looked quite pleased by it.

"Is it from the Pact of Hollowness?"

"No, the Whispers of Infinity."

Dysmas wanted to say more, but there was a chasm in his mind between thought and statement.

"I trust you to react to me," Prue said. "You're not like other men."

"And you're not like other women. I want to tell how, but—"

He stopped rowing, let the oars trail.

"It'd be a different *me* speaking, one from long, long ago."

"Then go ahead and tell me. If that's the *you* that speaks, that's the you that's here."

He studied her in the boat—beautiful now, she seemed, and a source of kindness to the imprisoned youth within him.

"You're a creature apart from this world, a pure form of living I'd like to be part of."

Slightly self-conscious, she inclined her face.

"Too bad we're in a rowboat," she said.

He raised the oars and they continued over the lake. Both of them were quiet and he sensed she was savoring the moment. She'd glance at him with half a smile, then look into the distance as if thinking of the future. What, he wondered, have I wrought? They came to a small inlet of the lake, heavily shaded and far now from the road. He sensed outdoor intimacy, watery nesting and secret, silent lives beyond human understanding. He let the boat slide onto the bank, pulled it further.

"This is my favorite spot," Prue said.

They climbed up the shore into the thickening trees and undergrowth. It appeared there would be just overgrown woods for a long way. Prue hastened on, though, and brought Dysmas to a clearing dominated by a massive, towering old tree.

"It's four to five hundred years," she told him.

There was a pond at one edge, ringed by round stones, and the greenish water appeared to be of even depth. Its surface reflected polygons of light, the late summer sun through overhanging branches. An old iron bench, heavily rusted, faced the pond and the great tree beyond it.

"Sit over there," said Prue. "I'll be back in a minute."

He assumed she was tending to some personal need. As he rested on the bench, absorbing the day's rising warmth, the pond he was facing seemed a giant birdbath, set in the ground to complement the giant tree. The width of the tree afforded ample concealment on the other side, which was why Prue had gone there, he thought.

There was a movement in the undergrowth, beyond the pond and beyond the old tree. The flash he'd seen was the size of a large fluttering bird. Maybe a nest in there, Dysmas guessed. But as he watched and caught the form again, he saw it was more solid, a mammal of some sort. It seemed to be both pale and dark, and it rose higher off the ground than he'd first noticed. It was floating through the thin upper reaches of undergrowth, a pale mammal with darker and wild hair, streaked with gray. As she came near the pond, eyes locking to his as she slowed, he saw that she was not a startled animal that would run away, though a part of him wished that she was.

Prue didn't smile at first but came gracefully through the last branches. She'd left her clothes beyond the tree, he saw, and her exposure was total. Her form absorbed his attention, cradled his youth in its curves. When she came to the pond, stepping over the ring of stones and scrambling the polygons on the surface, the light reflecting upward made patterns on her skin and she stopped to view them. She waded to the middle of the pond, watching the reflected light, then lowered herself. She knelt facing the sun, sat back, cocked an ear as if listening, then looked over at Dysmas and smiled.

He smiled back cautiously, at sea for a reaction. Prue looked back into sunny sky, bird calls from the lake now growing more audible.

"Do you like this?" she asked.

"Yes, very much."

"Can you come here, then?"

He rose from the bench and went to the ring of stones. He was surprised by his own composure. When he knelt at the edge of the pond, though, the appeal of her body was suddenly overwhelming. He felt dizzy, afraid he'd pitch forward into the water. He wondered if this could really be happening.

"Will you join me, Dysmas?"

"You mean—in there? With the same amount of clothes?"

"Yes. There's plenty of room, you know. I used to bathe here with Seniya."

The impulse to do it lasted less than a second. He realized at once how he'd look from the bench: onetime Brother Dysmas, sitting nude in a birdbath. No matter that no one would *be* on the bench. He could vividly imagine it himself.

"I don't think I can, Prue. I—"

"Don't worry about it, Dysmas. I accept you. I *want* you in here."

Her eyes were earnest. He allowed himself to meet them for a moment, sharing the vision. The hope in them was nurtured but he couldn't stand it because he knew it was doomed. He had to look away, with the same motion rising and turning from the pond. All he could do was walk away, leave the clearing and trudge back toward the boat. He abruptly did this, saying nothing and hoping that she wouldn't either. She didn't. He was well into the undergrowth and out of her sight when he slowed and let the panic ooze from him, the heat of frustration and regret taking its place. Then came the fear of Prue's reaction. Would she—did she now—feel humiliated? Rejected? Or would she somehow understand him and see no one was to blame? But, beyond all this, he knew that those needs remained that had led him to this place and that near-perfect woman in the pond.

She came down later, fully clothed, smiling just a bit self-consciously. Dysmas tried to be at ease, casual as before, but the weight of revelation was upon him.

"Thank you," he said. "I really mean it. Just understand it wasn't anything in *you* that kept it from happening. It was me. It *is* me—my particular craziness."

"But it *did* happen, Dysmas. So why should there be regrets? Never mind craziness."

"Well, I mean—"

"It did *happen*. We came to my special place and we had an honest, intimate experience. I'll always remember it."

She came the rest of the way to him, her eyes closing. She held his head and kissed him hard on the lips. Dysmas tried to respond, awkwardly holding the woman he'd abandoned in a pool. She was dear to him at this moment, almost precious, but he couldn't escape the thought of his walking away before, and the reason for it. He shouldn't *want* to forget, he knew. It wasn't rational. And she shouldn't, either. So however close they were, embracing here at Willowsong Lake, the knowledge of those limits had to haunt them, limit them. It was restriction that was beyond laws, beyond customs, in personal identities that evolved through decades. They were the most nebulous of barriers, and therefore the hardest to break.

8.

I was surprised, when Dysmas called, by his upbeat tone and his stated intention to stay at the Enneagram place beyond his planned retreat. He was fitting in there, it seemed. He'd even served as one of the moderators at a weekend retreat by a company. He hadn't lectured or led a discussion, per se, but he handled some exercises and chanting they did. He wasn't, of course, sold on the teachings of the place, but he saw nothing wrong with pretending he was so he could remain there. His decision to stay was apparently sealed by his hitting it off with Prue, the lead guru of the place. This led me to doubt the sustainability of Dysmas's choice, since relationships based on another's feelings are often ephemeral. This should have been apparent from his previous encounters, not to mention my own, but I let it pass since at least he was happy for a while.

Soon after his debut as a resident mentor, Dysmas noticed Edgar working in the vegetable gardens with retreaters from the yurts, their number grown to four. One had taken leave from the insurance company, being impressed by their retreat, and brought her female friend.

"Do you do this often?" Dysmas asked his colleague.

"As I'm inspired," Edgar replied drily. "Good for the soul, some say."

"Did you plow the furrows, too?"

"We have a helper for the heavy stuff, name of Regis."

"I haven't seen him."

"He lives in a shack on the river. Can't be around people much."

"A hermit?"

"Not quite. Just can't deal with women, tries to avoid them. There's no kind of vow involved, like we had. It's just a deep, controlling flaw in him. A hole in his soul."

A chill ran through Dysmas. He looked toward the unplanted

furrows beyond the laboring yurt dwellers. Regis's work, done no doubt in silence, stoically.

"That's too bad."

Edgar looked at him curiously.

"So, how did you find Willowsong Lake, with Prue?"

Was there, Dysmas thought, a hidden edge to the question? The cofounders nominally shared a bedroom in the house, but Edgar slept in a gable near Dysmas's.

"It was, I thought, beautiful. Inspiring."

"Better than the cave?"

"Well, what could ever top the Great Hollowness, that infinite potential?"

"Yes," Edgar smiled, "though it's the Great Stone Ring."

"Oh, yes. Of course."

As the days and then weeks passed, Dysmas saw little involvement in the counseling and activities afforded the retreaters, who continued to be few. Another group retreat was scheduled but then cancelled by the group without explanation. Prue remained enthusiastic, especially with the return of Seniya, who arrived one rainy evening to hugs from Prue and Dahlia. Edgar stood by noncommittally, Dysmas joining him in default reaction. Diamond remained in the servants' annex. Dysmas had encountered her on one of his visits to the dissolving stone cabin, surprising since Diamond had cryptically warned him that it was a "death cell." His visits had been to order his thoughts, but he saw Diamond came to smoke, a practice not tolerated near the house.

"Nice place for escape," he'd said, taking a stone slab seat.

She only smiled. Her slab was at a right angle to his.

"Have you worked here very long?"

"Too long."

"Come from England for the work?"

She eyed him, not quite suspiciously but maybe wondering how dense he was. She had dark brown hair cut short and an expression that was pert while smoking though blank when she was working.

"I come with the endowment."

"Endowment? What endowment?"

She matched his puzzled expression with her own.

"For the place, of course! You don't think it pays its own way, do you?"

Dysmas tried to understand but couldn't. He'd thought he was in the loop. Diamond seemed to soften, perhaps sympathize.

"I was with the Benefactor," she said. "He owns this place. You might see him sometime. Best keep your distance, though. Don't get involved."

Dysmas couldn't speak, didn't know what to say. Diamond threw down her cigarette, stubbed it out.

"I have to get back."

He was left in a state of incredulity, motionless on his stone seat in the ruin. He later began to realize that he should clear things up with the cofounders. Prue would have been the more approachable, normally, but soon she was fixated on Seniya, primarily the young woman's appearance. Tall and lissome, her clear features framed by long black hair, her effect on Prue seemed magnetic. That left Edgar, who'd remained somewhat distant with his suspicions about Willowsong Lake. Dysmas decided it best to follow Diamond's advice, at least for a while. Just wait and see, learn a little more before risking involvement.

In the meantime, he was curious about Regis, he who couldn't deal with women, tried to avoid them. Who had a deep, controlling flaw in him, according to Edgar—a hole in the soul. For Dysmas, echoes from his past were awakened by Edgar's words, the succinct conclusion a metaphorical shock. In his idleness and slipping confidence in the Center for Enlightened Culture, he felt moved to seek Regis out, or at least observe him in his natural habitat. He'd seen him a couple of times at the Center, digging post holes and moving machinery around the shed, but that was in his helper role, artificial like Dysmas's. The true Regis would be seen on his home turf.

On both trips to the special places of Prue and Edgar, they'd crossed a bridge over the minor river on which Regis lived. Dysmas took advantage of a pleasant autumn morning to have a longer than usual walk to this juncture. On reaching it, he observed the riverbank to be more heavily wooded upstream than down, so he judged that Regis must live downstream, where there'd be more space for a dwelling. On hiking along the bank for a goodly distance, however, and with an empty vista ahead, he decided that he'd been wrong. He retraced his route, crossed the road, and continued upstream. The going became rough and Dysmas was tussling with some pesky brambles when he finally sighted an anomaly ahead on the opposite bank. Crouched within dense forestland, the structure was low and long with grayish walls and corrugated green roof. Trying to ignore the stings of his prickly camouflage, Dysmas inched forward for a better look.

It appeared to be an old prefabricated storage shed, so close to surrounding trees that, with the green roof, it would be invisible from above. Towards the rear was the old pickup truck that Regis drove to the Center. There were cases of empty beer bottles stacked along a side, a deerskin drying on a rack in front, a rifle set against the wall nearby, and a boy about fourteen smoking a cigarette. He reclined with legs crossed in a plastic chair, one of three that were set facing the river. Dysmas, squatting in the brambles, envied the boy's comfort. As he watched, a second boy somewhat younger came through the screen door. He joined the older boy and they conversed with occasional laughter. It was a weekday, Dysmas considered, so schools would be in session. He was reminded of Leonid, the boy laborer at Pete's Perennials, education limited to Spanish phrases from a playmate. Dysmas's own education had been spotty, he knew, and it was partly his own fault, but at least he hadn't fallen through the cracks like these others.

Quietly, letting no branch swing free, he backed away and retreated toward the road.

⚫—◦—⚫

As the winds sweeping in from Canada and the Dakotas grew increasingly chill, counseling and activities at the Center were mostly conducted indoors. Larger spaces in the old motel and the house replaced the gardens and special places. The intake of clients for the Center diminished but, despite this and Seniya's return, Dysmas saw his role increase. The returned mentor was often involved with Prue in their personal activities, including daytrips to town, with Edgar left to fill in for his cofounder. Dysmas was thus left as the main counselor and guide to enlightenment. His guidance consisted simply of reading from the library's Enneagram materials, supplemented as much as possible with exercise and chanting.

"Hopefully, this situation is only temporary," Edgar said to him.

They were in a small office near the rear entrance to the house. Edgar was seated at the lone desk, normally Prue's station.

"Hopefully?" Dysmas queried.

"They were separated awhile. They're readjusting. Then we'll be back to normal as before."

In the process of adjusting, Seniya had co-opted Edgar's spot in Prue's bedroom.

"Normal," Dysmas repeated. "With a normal flow of retreaters, you think? Seems to be at a steady low these days."

"Well, we're coming into winter now, less interest in traveling for retreats. We can be doing road lectures, though. Visiting companies, community centers, et cetera."

"Same amount of proceeds from that?"

"Unfortunately, no. But anyway, we have the endowment. Maybe you've heard."

"Yeah, I think someone mentioned it once."

"As a matter of fact, Mr. Hagerstrom—he's our benefactor—will be stopping by soon. He'll be arranging a retreat for some associates. With Prue. He prefers just a single contact here."

"Do I get to shake his hand?"

"Actually, no. I'm glad you asked. He's averse to physical contact."

Dysmas was silent. Here it was, yet another individual to process.

"But don't worry about him. We'll have plenty to do taking care of his friends."

Dysmas was the only functioning mentor on the day of the Benefactor's arrival, cutting short one of his banal sessions upon hearing of the great man's presence. He proceeded to the larger parlor where other staff had gathered in docility. He found a tall man speaking in a voice so soft that Dysmas couldn't understand him or categorize his accent. He had salt-and-pepper hair slicked straight back and wore a gray business suit, as did his apparent secretary or assistant who sat with an attaché case in his lap. Prue was gazing in awe upon the speaker so did not notice Dysmas's entry and no introduction was given. The Benefactor himself gave the new mentor a single blank look and then continued his cryptic mumbling. Rather abruptly he turned toward Prue and gestured toward the rear of the house, location of the office, and walked out to it with her and the other gray business suit. Dahlia began to politely applaud but no one joined in so she stopped.

"They don't include you on the business end?" Dysmas inquired of Edgar. "A cofounder of the place?"

"Hagerstrom prefers Prue," the other man replied irritably. "Single contact."

"Oh, yeah. I forgot. It just seemed you were the one into finances."

"Prue can get him the raw info. His accountant can handle it from there."

"Accountant? Oh. I suppose he'll notice some big losses lately. Retreaters dwindling."

Edgar gave an ironic smile.

"Not to worry, Dysmas. I expect he'll cushion us with endowment funds so we look great. We'll get our dividends all right, and maybe higher than usual. We have that special group that's coming, Hagerstrom's friends. The books can project a big profit on that."

"Yeah? Wow. Thanks for explaining that to me, Edgar."

The cofounder smiled as he gazed upon the huge enneagram symbol in front of the window. Prue soon rejoined them from her conference, the men in gray suits leaving quietly by a rear doorway. The planning for the special retreat had been rather simple, it turned out, the Benefactor saying that about a dozen people would be arriving in two groups, one on the second day, with the motel residence their only quarters. Any others staying there should be relocated. Prue didn't mention any discussion or collaboration on financial matters, though there'd been ample time for such.

The weekend for the Benefactor's retreat was seasonably cold. A veneer of overnight snowflakes glistened in Friday's dawn as Dysmas viewed it from his gable window. There too, however, the ubiquitous funnel of factory smoke in the distance, starker for its contrast with the whiteness. Dysmas descended two floors to the kitchen, where Dahlia was beginning to get breakfast, assisted by her sister recruited for the special event. The ex-monk took his coffee to the front parlor window, peered out toward the motel residence. He'd supervised a deep cleaning of it by Regis and Diamond the day before. He decided to inspect it again after breakfast, today's retreat being of some great importance, apparently.

The facility, he later found, was pristine to the point of sterility, though hard to imagine as a venue for something momentous. He felt satisfied, notwithstanding. The mentors took turns staying in the motel residence by way of welcome, but the afternoon passed and evening was closing in by the time a dark van pulled into the motel parking area. Dysmas watched from his parlor window as the driver and two other men got out and began unloading passengers from the rear of the vehicle. Seniya came out from the motel and spoke with one of the men, gesturing toward the house as if explaining who was in charge. Edgar, who was in the parlor with Dysmas, rushed off to alert Prue and they were soon hustling down the drive to meet the arrivals. Dysmas remained at his window, noticing that the passengers leaving the van after the three men were all women. They appeared to be quite young in the light from the motel windows. They were seven in number, all but one with their possessions in bundles or shopping bags, the exception having a small suitcase. They were ushered into the motel by two of their escorts, Seniya following. Prue and Edgar lingered outside with the third man, discussing something in earnest.

Dysmas had the uncomfortable but familiar feeling of being in something over his head. He backed away from the window and its enneagram symbol, robotically crossed to the staircase, ascended two floors to his gable, and flopped face first onto his humble bed.

He awoke perhaps 45 minutes later, his mind a swirling fog that had threatened to reveal a nightmare. He had to get up, he knew, so he did. He would deal with things, he told himself. He was done with running. He returned to the staircase and carefully descended to where he found Seniya at the dining room table, eating alone though the other places were set. He took a seat diagonal to where she sat, inspected the covered serving dishes, found a pasta dish and steamed vegetables. He removed a French dinner roll from the basket and took a huge bite. Seniya pushed the wine bottle in his direction, her lovely face expressionless as she chewed.

"They're still out there," she said. "There's a problem with the delivery. They're a couple of girls short."

"There should be nine, then? For the retreat?"

Seniya gave him a blank look.

"Yeah, right. Though maybe it's ten there should be, a round number. So it's two or three they're short. I'm not sure."

She went on eating, savoring the pasta. Dahlia appeared in the doorway.

"Y'all need more of anything?"

Seniya gestured at Dysmas, who declined. He bit into the bread again, poured himself some wine, quaffed it. The Last Supper came to mind.

"I don't see where there's an issue," he said to Seniya. "Seems we could just go ahead with the retreat and bill the sponsor for the retreaters who are here instead of the number we expected."

Seniya stopped chewing and gave him an extended stare, blank again at first but melting into an amused smile.

"Yes, that would be logical. Would be, that is, if they were retreaters."

She hesitated as if awaiting his reaction, but Dysmas could only frown, wondering yet beginning to fear whatever she was talking about.

"You're not being disingenuous with me, are you?" she asked.

"No."

"Well, then. You see, those men with the girls are their handlers. As far as payment goes, that went where it was going yesterday by way of the endowment account, less a fee for services rendered."

Dysmas absorbed her statements silently, sorting things out in his mind. He could only get so far, though, before returning to the thought that he was in over his head. What, if anything, could he do about it? Sitting here with Seniya, wanting to appear under control, not befuddled, all he could think of was to eat. He accordingly heaped pasta and steamed vegetables onto his plate and emptied the wine bottle into his glass.

"Guess we'll need more of that," his companion laughed. "Be right back."

While she was gone, it occurred to him clearly that he had to get out of this place. Besides the current development, the flimsiness of his rationale for staying here was glaringly evident. He'd been extremely stupid and now it had landed him in something worse. He laid down his fork and sat with elbows on table and hands raised in a steeple, staring hard ahead at nothing in particular. He was still in this position as Seniya returned with the fresh bottle.

She hesitated before sitting and gave him another of her interested looks.

"Everything okay?" she asked.

"The food is fine," he responded.

She refrained from asking why he wasn't eating it then. She poured herself a drink and nibbled on fragments of bread as she observed him in his tense position.

"You don't like it here much, do you?"

He glanced over at her, thought a bit before he spoke.

"Just now, no."

"You mean—I take it you mean—with what's going down out there."

"Yeah."

"I don't either." She hesitated, then: "What about ongoing—the whole setup, process, the stuff they preach? Us, too."

Dysmas looked over at her, wondered why she was questioning him. It didn't matter, he decided. He was done with this garbage. This was just a random person he could talk with about it, release some of the pressure within himself, the mounting frustration with disappointments. If he chose to talk, that was. If he himself wanted to. He wasn't sure he did.

"I got fed up with it once myself," Seniya went on. "That was my 'leave of absence,' as they called it. I was thinking I wouldn't come back, but I couldn't find any place good enough, sure enough, to go. So back I came to here, to Prue."

She awaited his reaction. He gave a reassuring nod; he'd heard her.

"Security," he said. "You stayed for the security. That was my reason, too. Only I'm not sure there is any, unless you're in love with the Enneagram. Like these retreaters, some of them."

"They're just dupes, foolish people who'd believe anything that promised them bliss."

"That sounds a little harsh."

"Yes, it's a harsh business. Like what's going down tonight."

She gave a head tilt toward the motel residence, the people inside, the predicament. Her hair reflected the overhead light, more lustrous than Dysmas had noticed. It framed her face softly, enhancing its beauty. He was conscious of memories stirring in the deepest recesses of his mind. He poured himself more wine, then some for her, decided he was tired of talking, drained his glass.

"Guess I've had enough to eat," he said.

Seniya smiled, gave him a searching look.

"You can hide out if you want. I'll cover for you."

"Would you? That would be great."

He got up to leave, gave a woozy wave as he rounded the table, had almost left the room when she called his name, gestured him to the chair beside her.

"If you really want to go," she said, "you'd best do it right away, tonight. You'll be in trouble once they catch on to your thinking, our 'colleagues' or our visitors. They couldn't just let you go, maybe blab about what's going on here."

"You're talking actual physical harm?"

"The worst. You know they have guns, and we're outside the law here. Lots of forest and waterways to hide any evidence in."

It occurred to Dysmas that there'd been previous mentors at the Center who were never discussed, but he couldn't pursue that now.

"So how do I get away?" he asked instead.

"I can help you," Seniya responded, then looked away as if figuring how. "It'll have to be in the middle of the night, say three to four a.m. Get your things together and be ready to go. I'll tap on your door and we'll sneak out to my car very quietly. If it looks like I'll be stuck with Prue, I'll get Diamond to drive you."

"You think she'll do it? I thought she wasn't on good terms with you."

"That's just a ruse, so Prue won't suspect our relationship."

"Oh. I guess there's a lot I didn't know here."

"Just focus on your escape."

<hr />

It was Diamond who tapped on his door at 3:45 a.m., so lightly he thought it might just be a mouse. But there she was, finger to lips to warn against speaking. They carefully passed Edgar's door and slowly descended the stairways past Prue's. Seniya would be in there too, Dysmas thought, if she weren't posted at the motel residence. Departure from her without farewell momentarily bothered him. Diamond was noiseless on the wooden steps, but Dysmas with his small suitcase occasionally raised a faint creak.

Seniya's car was a small sedan similar to Prue's. Diamond pulled away at once upon gaining ignition, forbearing any warmup to minimize their noise. She drove slowly down the driveway to the turn onto the road, Dysmas noticing lights in the motel office but unable to see who was posted there. They rode mostly in silence along the lightless road, Diamond not seeming drowsy but intent upon her task.

"I really appreciate your doing this for me," Dysmas said. "You and Seniya."

"She's paying me."

"Oh. Well, still I'm grateful to you."

Diamond reached into her jacket pocket.

"Here. She said to give this to you."

Dysmas unfolded the sheet of paper. It was the address of someone named Samuel in San Jose, California.

"In case you get desperate for somewhere to go," Diamond explained.

"Thank you. And thanks to Seniya."

When they arrived in town, they stopped at an all-night café near the bus depot. Dysmas ordered breakfast and offered to treat Diamond, but she settled for coffee and a cigarette.

"I have to get right back," she said. "Regular workday ahead."

She was soon gone in Seniya's car while Dysmas continued his meal. He took his time, lingering in the café since the depot was not yet open. Reviewing his sudden departure, he tried to verify for himself that he'd done the right thing, not acted rashly from impulse or misinformation. It seemed that he had, but then why was he sitting here with his future again a blank slate, with little to nothing gained, apparently, from his latest sojourn? It was part of a larger pattern, he suspected, perhaps the one described by the nun who'd said he'd make a wonderful priest.

"You cannot refuse a calling to Holy Orders," she'd said. "If you try, you will never be happy in any other situation in life. The unaccepted calling will haunt you."

He related this thought to me later when he telephoned from the depot. I was glad to hear from him and supported his departure from the Center, but on the Divine calling I could offer no opinion. He seemed to understand.

9.

Upon learning of my engagement, Dysmas declined my offer of shelter in our condo. I therefore told him I'd stake him to a month's residence in an extended stay motel. He thanked me but again declined, said he had enough money but wasn't sure he'd be returning to our city. Too many things had gone wrong for him here and he didn't think that he belonged. He'd mull it over on his bus ride, he said, then decide where to go at the train station in Minneapolis.

When I hadn't heard from Dysmas for several weeks, I called his sister Lucy out at Pete's Perennials. She said they'd received a holiday card from Dysmas that was postmarked Lakewood, Colorado. He was just passing through, however, writing that he was going to check out Taos, New Mexico, having read about it in an article about D.H. Lawrence. I began to check with directory assistance in that town from time to time, but was always told he was not listed.

Months passed. I'd been promoted to senior management at my firm and was busy there and with my fiancée on our wedding and honeymoon plans. Tracking down Dysmas became lower in priority for me. I reasoned that he could and would contact me if he needed my assistance in any way. This seemed logically correct, but I should have given more weight, perhaps, to his demonstrated lapses in judgment. About nine months after we'd last spoken, I received a call from Brother Samuel at the No Lost Souls Mission in San Jose, California. He was calling in regard to Dysmas.

"You were listed as an emergency contact," Samuel explained.

"Yes, I've known him since childhood."

"You were very close, then."

"Were? Yes, we still are as far as I know. Though I've recently lost touch with him."

I felt some anxiety stirring. Samuel sighed at the other end.

"I must inform you that your friend is deceased."

103

"Dysmas died? Are you sure? How did it happen? Where?"

"We all extend our sympathy, those of us here and those at our monastery up north, past Sacramento. That's where Dysmas passed away. He was transferred there after an incident here in San Jose."

"What was the cause of death?"

"Something called hemochromatosis. It's an abnormal buildup of iron in the body, not fatal if treated in the early stages, but Dysmas disregarded the symptoms. There's darkening of the skin, fatigue, joint pain. He thought they all came from his labor outside. The monastery is on a regular working farm."

"Did anybody else there contract it?"

"It's not contracted. It's hereditary, in the DNA."

"You mentioned an incident that got him sent there."

"Yes, he broke up a Mass. A Catholic church service."

"I don't understand."

"He went up the center aisle in a church with his arms raised, got to the altar and told the priest he should stop the service. That he, Dysmas, would save everyone directly. In other words, that he was Christ, God."

I sat mutely in my armchair, feeling cut off from the world, from reality.

"I'm sorry, Brother Samuel. I'm feeling rather overwhelmed by all this."

"Yes, I can understand. But I have a photo of your friend that I can send you. It's likely the last one taken of him. He's standing outside with someone who came to join him at the monastery. She was comforting to him at the end. I can get the picture off to you in tomorrow's dispatch."

"Thank you. I'd greatly appreciate it."

I was distracted in my work and with my fiancée for the next several days, but I'd recovered from my initial shock by the time Samuel's envelope arrived. The photo showed Dysmas standing outdoors with a spade in one hand and his opposite arm around an attractive dark-haired young woman. Both were wearing work clothes and smiling widely at the camera. On the photo's reverse was inscribed a succinct caption: *Seniya and Dysmas*. I studied the picture for signs of ill health but saw none in either party.

There was a note from Samuel enclosed with the photo. It read:

Here is the photo of Dysmas with my grandniece. She is currently carrying his child. Your friend suggested you could help them when he was gone. He said you were always there for himself when he needed assistance.

I reached for my whiskey drink and took a generous swallow. From the kitchen came sounds of my prospective wife preparing a tasty dinner for us. We'd be having an interesting conversation at the table, I foresaw.

THE THIRD VENTURE

1.

During an all-Mozart program at the Sydney Opera House, a phone vibrated in the suit coat of a man seated near an exit. The man, Ian Newcombe, observed the caller's number and knew he should leave to call back. Reluctant to leave his party, he considered waiting for intermission. His respect for urgency intervened, however, so he whispered regrets to his wife and discreetly exited.

Entering the hall, Newcombe was highly visible to any who might be there. He was six-foot-five and 240 pounds, with broad shoulders and steel-gray hair worn longish. He was thus spotted by a man who was ambling unsteadily from the direction of the bar. Newcombe vaguely recalled the man from business luncheons, but wasn't sure of his name. Was it Reynolds? Raymond? Mediocre people were just globs after a time.

"Late from intermission," the man explained. "Wife'll be ticked." His face had a cherubic look, his wispy moustache not lessening it.

"Another's coming soon," Newcombe advised. "You can slip back in."

"Eh? Oh, yes." He seemed sloppily thoughtful.

"Well, if you'll excuse me—"

"Say, I wanted to ask you something."

"Yes?"

The man smiled conspiratorially, Newcombe returning a poker face.

"I hear your stock's shot up since you landed Kenilwerth."

The man was referring to the Progress Island venture, which Newcombe had launched when another firm collapsed there. They'd been into life extension, while Newcombe's success was in derivatives, but he was a dilettante of the first order.

"We're not issuing shares yet."

"Good. Glad of that, actually." The man suddenly seemed sober. "Let me in the group, Ian. I can stake as much as any of them."

Newcombe hesitated, judging the man, then: "Group's closed for now. The others would have to agree. I'll bring it up with them and let you know."

With that he briskly moved on. The familiar feeling of being a stallion running with geldings returned to him. But he knew that no man was an island, not if he wanted any real success. There were networks and systems to work through, resources to be negotiated, meeting and dealing and wining and dining. He'd seen this starkly one bleak afternoon as he perched atop a Himalayan peak, watching as frigid gales swept over the immense, timeless crust. He was nothing, he realized, and neither was any man on earth, past or present, no matter how strong or brilliant. It was only by working with others, or using others, as well as human institutions, that he would be of any significance. And so he resisted his loner impulse, continually alert to the business environment, seeking engagement, and he assumed this outlook in other areas as well. He willingly patronized the arts, though he didn't understand them, and the sciences which he appreciated more. He saw science as the key to progress, with which he naturally identified, and thus had been drawn to the legacy of Progress Island. He came to an empty alcove and ducked in, reconnected with his recent caller.

"They're sending a researcher from WHO," the voice said.

"Investigator, you mean."

"If you will. New fellow there, bit of a break maybe."

"Name?"

"David Pons. Know him at all?"

"Hm, no. When can we expect Mr. Pons?"

"Better think tomorrow. Is your manager good for this?"

Newcombe frowned in thought, people passing his alcove.

"Andrew's fine with pressure, got through that other project. But I think more precision is needed on this. Diplomacy. A productive handling of the visitor."

"Want us to fly someone in?"

"No, I think I'll go myself. I'd like to turn this to our advantage. Get us off the defensive in the larger picture."

"I'm with you, Ian."

———•———

Livia was listening to a radio broadcast of the concert from Sydney. She was in her apartment in the capital of the kingdom of which Progress Island was a part. As the orchestra's efforts filled her living room, Livia paged through some work she'd brought home from her office at the Ministry of Culture. It concerned a proposal to form a touring company of musicians from the Kingdom. Being deputy minister, Livia would be expected to provide meaningful and perhaps decisive input.

Though she was nearing fifty, Livia appeared to be only in her mid-thirties. This was due to her receiving an artificial chromosome from an earlier effort on Progress Island. She had long black hair, naturally wavy, and a light golden complexion. Her American husband had received the chromosome earlier, but he'd returned to his homeland, not wanting to live indefinitely in the Kingdom. They had only been visiting, actually, but Livia found she was still as popular as when she'd emigrated. In addition, there'd been a government purge and the new regime had offered a big promotion from her previous work. The country was a constitutional monarchy, with the royals' authority now much diminished.

The phone rang on the table next to Livia. It was her sister Mona, who lived in another part of the main island. Their other relatives lived on the outlying smaller islands.

"I'm worried about Cora," Mona said. She was referring to her daughter, the youngest of her three children.

"It's getting worse?"

"No, the same. But she's getting older, fourteen now. So compared with other girls, their activities and all, it shows up more. That lack of stamina. It holds her back so."

"And you see it more than anyone, being her mother. Yes, of

course I sympathize. But you've done all you can, Mona. The doctors, all those tests. They didn't find *anything*?"

"No, everything normal, supposedly. But you know, Livia, one of them hinted there was maybe something hereditary. So I told him about aunt Cow-Eyes, but then he said that it wasn't his field."

"He didn't want to deal with Cow-Eyes, just as no one wanted to before. She was a puzzle, it's true, and quite a burden for people."

The sisters were referring to their great-aunt Xenia, who would spend most of the day in bed with no apparent malady. She never married or performed any useful work.

"Oh, Livia! To think Cora might end up like *that*!"

"Now, Mona. Cora's not anywhere close to what Xenia was. There was probably something psychological, and at that time–"

"But what if there wasn't? What if it's in our genes–gender linked and skipping generations?"

Livia hesitated, Mona having pressed into a delicate area. Her concern must have grown intense to so override her discretion.

"Well, I'm not really an expert on it just because–well, that was different, Mona."

"You have the contacts though, Liv. You know the people out there."

"What, you mean Progress Island?"

"Yes."

"But it's much different now, Mona. Most of the *people* are different, and there's those clones. They're not really seeking immortality anymore, just trying to guarantee health through genetic manipulation, with life extension secondary."

"Yes. Yes, I know."

Livia saw that she'd strengthened her sister's position, clarifying what Mona was hoping to get for Cora with Livia's assistance.

"I don't know," she said. "I don't see how I'd approach them, or how Cora would fit in with what they're doing now. It's all experimental, Mona."

"But you could find out–right, Liv? You're a deputy minister and they're foreigners here, even though they're autonomous. You have some *authority*."

"I can't use it for personal gain though, including for family. Remember the purge?"

"There must be some way, though. At least to get information, to see what's possible. Can't you go through someone else?"

Livia saw that she'd have to make the effort.

"I love Cora too, Mona. I'll check around."

———◆———

Returning from the hotel's VIP dining room, David Pons lingered over a view of Manila. A sea of lights, as in other cities, but seemingly less intense here. Perhaps the humidity, he mused, or actually less power. He was a bit below average height, slender, with sallow complexion and dark blond hair, floppy though it was trimmed short. He was 26 years old and held a master's degree in anthropology.

David was stopping over on his way to Progress Island, his assignment from WHO. He'd checked in at the Manila office but received a cool reception. It was understandable, he decided. His study was within their district and rather close to them, so why was he–an apparent lightweight–being sent all the way from Geneva? But David little cared what they thought. He'd serve the higher authority.

He proceeded along the corridor to his room, recalling the sunlit window behind Dr. Shashamene at his desk.

"I want *you* on this, David," he'd said, "because I want the wider scope. Not too much focus on medical technicalities. A more general view of the situation is needed–the history of the island, the cultures involved, the politics of the Kingdom, and–well, the moral direction."

"Moral direction, sir?"

"Not in the religious sense, of course. There's already oversight on that from fanatics the world over. But we must ascertain the purpose, the central values, of the people driving this effort, this project and its ramifications. Where do they honestly place the welfare of humanity among their priorities?"

"I see, sir. I'll make that my central inquiry."

"It should help that you have a contact there. The manager of the island facility, in fact. Remember Andrew? From the conference when you started with us."

"Yes, I believe I do. Yes, that should definitely help. I can apply myself more closely. More thoroughly."

Dr. Shashemene had smiled.

"Good! That's another reason I'm assigning you, David: your seriousness. I'm impressed with your dedication."

David well knew that, in his values, he was an idealist. Since this often put him at odds with others of his generation, he could sometimes feel anachronistic. In his assessments of situations, however, and his approach to solutions, he was coldly realistic. The idealism rested in his desired end results. This had impressed the recruiter from WHO and, together with David's references, had sealed the position for him. His personal history hadn't hurt, either. He'd lost his father in childhood and lived with his mother and younger sister, yet excelled as a student as far as he'd wished to go. He was apolitical and non-religious, had no "significant other" and few friends. He was thereby free to work assiduously at his job.

He unlocked his room with the plastic card, entered and switched on a light, enjoyed the sensation of entering a private place, which was always relaxing for him.

"Perhaps a little more wine?" he spoke aloud, and crossed to the mini-fridge.

He poured the Cabernet into a clear plastic tumbler, regretting he hadn't brought his glass from the dining room. He took a sip and reflected on whether he was happiest in hotel rooms. No, he decided, the little apartment in Geneva was better, despite his vulnerability there, the lack of anonymity. One had some need for familiarity, a settled haven, no matter how flexible one was. Yet he could easily step away from it and function fully on the road, he thought, and he meant to demonstrate it on this assignment.

He carried his wine to the small balcony outside his room, through sliding glass doors. Another view of the city lay below him.

"Behold," he said, "all this I will give to thee," and briefly smiled.

No, he answered within himself, I have no need of your seedy delights. They're of no interest to me. They're separate from my existence, my functioning and affirmation. My empowerment. And his thoughts turned to Progress Island, its people, its clones. An energy gathered within him, facilitated by wine, narrowing his focus to the coming strategy: intense scrutiny, dissection, mastery of any and all involved. His report would be comprehensive, incisive, flawless.

"I'll ride through the valley of darkness," he proclaimed, "and it will be mine."

2.

Nameless and unused through most of history, Progress Island gained fame as a venue for experiments in life extension. First through altered and artificial chromosomes, then through cloning with mind implantation, the ultimate goal was always immortality. Now, in its third incarnation as scientific utopia, life extension was downplayed in favor of high *quality* in living. This gave Newcombe Ventures a more positive aura than its predecessors. Over time, of course, goals could be adjusted in response to commercial factors.

The island retained its autonomous status under a nearby island kingdom. The government of the Kingdom, a constitutional monarchy, still smarted from the purge triggered by a scandal with the first life extension project. To forestall more upheaval after the second failure, the government accepted a proposal offered by Newcombe Ventures. The island and its resident clones were purchased, with the provision that the Kingdom be privy to operations. An official liaison was named and the country was to share in the project's benefits.

A number of new structures had been erected on the island for the latest project. Beyond the ribbon of forest behind the cove cottages, a dining and recreation building had risen above the rocky shallows of the southern coast. There were tennis courts adjoining this building to the north, then open meadow extending to the dock on the northern coast. East of the meadow, in the scientific compound, a large new lab had been added to the south of the existing buildings. This was needed to serve the medical needs of the clones and included special equipment to test their development in various areas. Further to the south, not far from the dining and recreation building, an education center had been built. Finally, on the fin-like northeast corner of the island, a guard building now stood. The hill on the southeast corner would have seemed more practical, but the psychological impact on clones and visitors had to be considered.

Andrew, the project manager, chose to reside in the old staff residence within the compound. It was close to the office on the northern end, where his presence was expected. Others, including Dr. Shah, chose to live in some cove cottages not used for clones. Andrew and Dr. Shah had worked together in the preceding life extension project, though they'd had little control and were not at fault for its failure. Their experience was thus of value to Newcombe Ventures. They also worked congenially as a team, frankly discussing any issues requiring leadership.

"Well," Andrew was saying, "I guess this was bound to happen sooner or later. It's certainly sooner than I expected, though." He was nearing forty, trim and clean-shaven with light brown hair.

"Yes," Dr. Shah responded, "our monitors and instruction on prophylaxis should have precluded it." He was short with a round face, dark hair combed flat to the side.

"For a scientific project, it might indicate a lack of controls, a chance occurrence that will influence our findings. Should we terminate like with the others?"

"Well," the doctor smiled, "no one need know it's unintended. And the child could be very useful to us, allow a quick start on our research of offspring."

Andrew thought a moment.

"It's not like those others, I suppose–from that out-of-control situation."

"Wandering like animals," Shah nodded.

They were referring to the scene they'd inherited on the island, untended clones making their own erratic way, following their basest instincts. Two abortions had been performed.

"Do we know the father?" asked Andrew.

"I'll be taking saliva samples from the males. We'll compare their DNA to foreign DNA fragments in the mother's bloodstream– that is, fragments from the fetus." Shah grinned. "The smart money's on Kittridge."

Andrew returned a smile. The clone in question was a frisky male who'd been carrying the name of his donor, a successful but elderly businessman.

"We'll have to rename him soon. Legal precautions. But, on the DNA matching, you've talked to Noelle about it?"

"She's my next stop. Actually, I think she'll be able to map a complete genome."

"For the fetus?"

"Yes."

"And from there–pre-natal enhancement?"

Dr. Shah raised a cautionary hand.

"I'd wait on that for a pairing of our selection. And supervision. We can then have full control. This case can give us a run-through on procedures, though. Some practice."

"And, if there are genetic defects?"

"We should just observe, I think, save ourselves–save Noelle–for the real work ahead. She does have her limits, after all, despite her enhanced nature."

"Yes, I suppose so. And we know she's the key to things now, at least for the company."

Dr. Noelle Kenilwerth had just recently come to work for Newcombe Ventures. She'd also been a key figure in the original work on the island, which focused exclusively on life extension. While she'd left that work with the project's collapse, she continued to benefit from it through an artificial chromosome designed and infused in her by her late husband. She thus could not escape the concept of genetic enhancement and was open to the supporting views of others. Despite some reservations, she was inclined to join the current project so that her expertise would fashion a greater good. It was a natural move for her, she thought, and no great sacrifice since she was to live for centuries.

As Andrew spoke with Dr. Shah, Noelle sat in one of the older labs, her original work station on the island. She had the appearance of a very young woman, petite with wavy black hair and pale skin. She was studying the genomes of the island's clones, mostly developed under her predecessor in the second project. A few clones had still been gestating and so were unfinished products. Noelle saw a great deal of work ahead, especially since the project's goals went far beyond physical matters to mental and social development. The behaviors of all the clones would have to be closely monitored with constant reference to their genetic make-ups and alterations. Enhancements had to be timely, compatible, and maximally effective.

Noelle opened a desk drawer, took out a stack of notebooks, opened the top one to a random page. She studied the hasty writing, the diagrams, imagined the writer's motions and smiled.

"Terence," she whispered, "it should be you sitting here."

She proceeded to page through the notebooks as she often did, seeking inspiration for her work. She was aware that, officially, life extension was secondary in the work here. But it must be a rather close "second" for them to seek her out, there being many others working in genetic improvement. The corollary goal of a 140-year lifespan had been mentioned. They would eventually want more, she knew, since the market would and this was a commercial enterprise. Still, with other enhancements improving the *quality* of life, eventually for whole societies, this use of Terence's work was more justified than the first time around.

"Yes," she nodded to the notes, "this will be your legacy, your redemption."

The water taxi bringing David Pons arrived in late afternoon. He was met by Andrew and Dr. Shah, along with a helpful clone who wanted to carry David's bag.

"Thank you, no."

"It's all right," said Andrew. "He enjoys it."

"I'd rather take it myself."

"Sure thing. Back to the beach, Robert."

David watched curiously as the Adonis disappeared down the path to the cove.

"Our compound is this way," Andrew gestured.

They departed in the direction opposite to Robert's. A tropic buzz accompanied their steps on the dusty path, the ground rising as they neared the entrance to the compound, where an armed guard was posted. Little was said on the way.

"We'll get you settled," Andrew said, "then have some refreshments."

David was shown to a room in the old staff residence, where Andrew himself lived. Also staying in the residence was Ursula, a financial consultant from Newcombe Ventures, who'd arranged a light dinner to welcome David. She was in her thirties with golden hair cut fashionably short. She sat in with the men as eating gave way to discussion. They were in the lunchroom adjoining the project offices.

"We're flattered by your organization's interest," Dr. Shah was saying. "Our work here is still in an early experimental stage. Practical application is quite far off, if ever."

"And yet you conduct your procedures on human, or just humanoid, subjects."

"Humanoid, yes. Evolving, as it were, to the human."

David looked at him blankly. Ursula broke in with an office smile.

"They were roaming all over when police from the Kingdom came. They were ready to treat them like animals. Our company stepped in just in time."

"With our enhancements to their natures," Dr. Shah explained, "they can be educated, socialized, truly live as human beings. That's all I meant to say."

"You have professionals from those areas on your staff?"

"We currently bring teachers over from the Kingdom," Andrew spoke up. "As for social skills, Ursula is doubling as advisor to the caregivers."

David Pons looked skeptical.

"The Kingdom is a partner of sorts in our work," Ursula pursued. "There's an understanding they'll be among the first to benefit from our success. Our subjects here might be integrated into their society, become solid and productive citizens."

"The clones?"

"Yes!"

"Ah, along the way," injected Dr. Shah, "some genetic refinements will be made available to certain citizens over there. This will benefit their society and make them more receptive to the, ah, relocations from here."

"And for the world beyond the Kingdom?"

"I will submit to the medical journals, personally, all findings of use in combating major diseases and disorders."

David softened a bit, resembling more a guest.

"Well, that would certainly be welcome."

"We do admire your organization," said Ursula. "We'd like you to see us as partners for world health."

David didn't respond.

"Anything we can do to help," Andrew added, "in your study or later, feel free to ask. We have tight security, of course, but you have full access to our facilities and staff."

"Thank you."

The dinner at an end, Ursula returned to her office and Dr. Shah left for his residence on the cove. Andrew led David on a walk to the hill on the island's southeast corner, from which he could view the compound and more. Evening was settling in, a clear orange sky gradually fading to a tapestry of very bright stars.

"Is that a helipad?" David asked, looking toward the eastern shore.

"Yes. Little used now, but we keep it for medical emergencies."

David was thoughtful, then: "Dr. Shah, talking about findings, said you'd release any discoveries on major pathologies. Am I to understand, then, that it's only in minor areas, what you *consider* minor, that you'll be claiming trade secrets?"

Andrew hesitated, tried to imagine Ian Newcombe's response, couldn't do so.

"Well, I'm not a legal professional, but I expect that, being a business after all, we'd want to have proprietary rights for some processes we end up marketing. They could be important, be marketable, without involving major health issues. They might involve cosmetic changes, perhaps development of talents–"

"And maybe longevity? Life extension?"

Andrew picked up the pace.

"Hopefully people will live longer–and better–from *all* the work we do here. But I know what you're getting at, David. We're fortunate enough to have Dr. Kenilwerth on our staff. Actually, though, she has a *range* of experience in her field. She's spent the last few years on research into those major pathologies. I'm sure she'll be happy to tell you directly about her work, both past and present."

They ascended the hill under the dimming sky, Andrew feeling pleased with how he was handling the situation.

3.

Because of Livia's acquaintance with the past of Progress Island, the Ministry of Culture considered it natural for her to monitor the current project. Their role wasn't on the level of medicine or commerce, but the project would eventually impact the Kingdom's society, so they needed to be prepared. Livia was content with music programs and the like, but she had no good reason to refuse the task. It also provided an approach to the island on behalf of her niece with the strange malady. As Mona had suggested, she could go through someone else to avoid any ethical questions, and Livia had duly sifted through her contacts. By far the most effective would be the police liaison to the project, Lt. Col. Troy Duillu.

Like Livia, Troy was from an outlying smaller island of the Kingdom. This had at first hampered his career with the national police, but the government purge had extended to their department and opened doors for him. He was almost a decade younger than Livia but, because of her genetic change, Troy appeared a little older. He was strikingly handsome and retained a sunny disposition he'd found useful during his struggling years. He had a natural attraction that made Livia reluctant to work with him, she valuing her marriage and professional standards. But now there was Cora's illness to handle and, as she found when she met Troy for lunch, other imperatives as well.

"So," he said after small talk, "Progress Island?"

"Yes. We've never really discussed it except in the committee."

"Well, we have different priorities. Though it's always nice to talk with you, of course."

Livia smiled but quickly went on.

"Have you had much contact with them recently? Do you go out there?"

"Actually landing? No, they have their own security, high quality it seems. I do have something coming up, though. The Commerce Ministry wants an escort for the CEO, Mr. Newcombe, when he visits out there. I'll be with him from the airport to the island, perhaps also on his return."

"Is something special happening?"

"Not really. It's just because someone from the World Health Organization is out there, doing some kind of inspection. I guess the CEO wants to talk with him."

"So you'll be out there awhile, then."

Troy shrugged.

"As long as I'm needed."

"And all the important staff will be around."

"Well, he *is* the CEO."

Livia hesitated a moment, then yielded to inspiration.

"Any chance I could go along?"

She'd asked with her old hostess smile. A look of pleasant surprise crossed Troy's face. He reached for his cigarettes, offered her one. She accepted though she was cutting down.

"Of course," Troy answered. "I know you have an interest in the place, along with your ministry. Come to think of it, you did this sort of work with the Commerce Ministry."

It had actually been more complicated, but Livia had put those days behind her.

"It'll make my current job much easier," she said. "I won't have to look like another WHO inspector keeping tabs on them. Plus, we'd sort of get to work together."

"Always a pleasure," Troy smiled through the smoke.

It was much better this way, Livia felt. She didn't have to review Cora's problem with Troy, getting him to understand and be motivated. She could work her way into the Progress Island circle more smoothly. Best of all, maybe, she needn't be indebted to Troy beyond the escort task. They'd remain just professional friends.

She could cover all her bases after all, Livia thought.

David Pons had had a full day on the island. Now, as night gathered after dinner, he descended the path to the docking area, reflecting. They'd given him a tour of the compound and outer buildings, explaining the functions of the facilities. Much of the equipment in the labs, especially the new one, was too arcane for his understanding. He didn't let on, of course. He'd been impressed with the education center, well equipped with computers and media, and the dining/recreation center as well. The clones themselves continued to mystify him, distracting him from his hosts as they showed him around the cove. He'd decided to have another look once night had fallen, when the clones were confined to their quarters.

Passing the dock, he continued on the path to Reverie Cove.

Andrew and Ursula had stressed the holistic treatment their project would offer both the individual and society. They were not simply producing beautiful people, they insisted. That was already possible, had been done. They were also concerned with the subject's internal development and interaction with society, and with societies themselves by improving the inherent capacities of their citizens. A given population would increase in quality people, especially as they had offspring. Granted, this would be through genetic enhancement, a process that was seen as artificial. But the end result would be a better natural world, as ideal as possible, and achieved using the intellect that is natural to humans. Their paradigm, therefore, was a natural solution to most of what troubled the world. David had nodded thoughtfully to all this, refraining from skepticism. It seemed they were on to him as an idealist.

He passed the northern point of the cove, the lower-numbered houses extending out toward the sea. At the end was number 1, larger and better built than most of the others, the residence of Dr. Shah. He and some others felt free to use the clones as servants, "for their own good," as David was told. He questioned the doctor as to whether clones were being deliberately bred for such specific roles, servile or otherwise.

"Of course not," Shah had answered. "We're in a research phase here, not applications, and certainly not making-to-order."

"Nevertheless," David countered, "by implanting certain characteristics, such as reduced aggression, you render them manipulable in a given direction."

"But we don't *seek* specific directions. The qualities with which they're enhanced give them access to a generally better life, and a better ability to live with others. Your example, reduced aggression, obviously helps with interpersonal relations and being a good citizen."

"You have no doubts about where your research may lead?"

"When doubts arise, we resolve them. It's all science."

Reaching the beach, David removed his shoes and walked southward in the sand. There was a path that fronted the houses, a ridge of firmer footing, but he wanted to avoid encounters and observe from a distance. The fine white sand was cool and oozed pleasantly between his toes. Above, the moon was full and already bright, stars in full abundance. He could see why this place had once been sought for retirement homes. Besides number 1, number 14 was also superior to the others, and a small house on the far point looked good too. That would be number 27, David figured. The tackier houses were either fully lit or totally dark, meaning they were either used or available for clones, while the nicer homes had normal, partial lighting.

He continued down the beach, coming to where it narrowed toward the southern point. He stopped before number 26, which was dark, and put on his shoes. He wanted to take a different route back, above the southern shore. As he left the beach and looked for passage through the houses, however, he saw Noelle reclining on the patio of number 27. She was holding a wine glass and looking southward over the sea. The light from the cottage fell behind her, leaving her mostly in just moonlight, yet her face and limbs were distinct and softly glowing. It was a strange luminescence David hadn't seen before, at least from a human being.

She noticed him and looked over, her eyes seeming to flash.

"Hi," she said, and lifted her glass. "Care for some wine?"

He'd talked with her briefly on his tour, but her replies to his questions had been stilted like those of the lesser staff members. He'd had the feeling she was holding back. Now, however, away from the others, she seemed entirely relaxed. It was he himself who had to deal with discomfort, steel himself against her strangeness.

"Thank you," he said, "I will."

He took a seat at the patio table as she went to fetch the wine. She returned with a glass for him and the bottle, then sat in a different spot than before, where light from the cottage reduced her strange glow.

"Long story," she said, touching her face.

Despite his role, David felt compelled to be gentle with her, a reaction that surprised him. As usual, however, he'd keep his personal feelings to himself.

"There were hazards in your work, I suppose."

"Yes."

Her eyes searched his features, her thoughts apparently elsewhere. David sipped his wine, an excellent Pinot Noir that itself would have justified the stop.

"I suppose," he said, "it was mostly your work in life extension that attracted Newcombe Ventures."

Noelle smiled serenely, totally different from her laboratory persona.

"Could be," she said.

"It's important to them, then, as part of the package they'll be marketing. Perhaps the *most* important part?"

"I don't know about 'most.' I can understand–"

Her eyes dropped to her wine, which she swirled a bit.

"I mean, I can see why people think that, why people want it. They always have."

She looked up and their eyes met directly, David again noting a sparkle in hers.

"Don't get me wrong," he said. "I admire your work, the good that you've done, and of course your courage."

Noelle shrugged.

"I wasn't alone."

She couldn't help searching his features again, his expressions. The edge in his voice and his persistence added to their effect on her, their evocation of Terence. He was saying something now about the future, about after their research, about societies, the world community.

"Would it be good then—that is, ethical—to provide a sort of immortality to countries based on their wealth? In striving for a perfect human strain, in selling the process to highest bidders, doesn't it encourage the notion of a nation–a race–of supermen?"

Beneath his manners was his intensity, Noelle saw, and felt a familiar warmth rising. She couldn't begin to deal with his question.

"Well–" she faked, frowning as if thoughtful. And after a hesitation: "Why don't we move inside, take some more comfortable chairs?"

She was moving while yet speaking; David had little choice but to follow. They passed through a room with a pool table to a drably furnished living room. David was attracted to a stack of esoteric magazines on the coffee table. He picked one up.

"Copper pipe fittings?"

"Previous resident," Noelle smiled. Another long story, she could have added. But it wasn't the one she wanted to tell tonight, not to this man who might already be picking up her feelings. She wanted him to know about Terence, understand him maybe, as well as why she was the way she was, and why she cared about him.

"I have some background on all this," she told him, and returned to her graduate research days–hers and Terence's. There were his early findings, the stolen credit, discouragement from going further. There was the censure, loss of funding, the compulsive persistence that led to self-experimentation. She'd been unable to help him in the end, was herself changed to something a creation apart from her original self. Yet his spirit was stamped on her own and she was dedicated to the fruition of his work, his vision. It was a gift to humanity that he'd died for.

"I think you're one who can understand," she said. "Aren't you?"

While her glow had receded in the artificial light, Noelle still exerted an allure on David. Her account of the other man had struck an unfamiliar chord in him. A remote part of his nature, unknown or ignored, had sensed kinship with her late husband, and its complement in the deep mystery of Noelle.

"Yes," he answered, then caught himself. Things were getting out of control. "But I really should be getting back now. Your CEO, Mr. Newcombe, is coming tomorrow and I should be rested for our meeting."

Noelle smiled and glanced toward a darkened adjoining room.

"Stay here. You'll rest like you never did before. I guarantee it."

David's resistance, any that existed, collapsed and melted away. Incredibly to his conscious self, he heard himself complying. His mind saw Dr. Shashamene, his superior, at his desk with the sunlit window behind. But soon that melted away as well.

4.

Having decided to meet personally with the WHO researcher, Ian Newcombe hired a free-lance journalist to report on his visit. The journalist wrote for business and consumer publications, as well as their Internet outlets, and was sometimes interviewed by broadcast media. Newcombe was uneasy about the researcher's presence and wanted to preempt any negative effects. At the same time, he thought he could prime the market for the project's eventual services.

"Now, Harry," he said on the plane, "you understand the story is contingent. You'll get your fee, of course, but if you can't put a positive spin it's no-go. The WHO can do their own disseminating."

The journalist, a neatly ordinary man, was nonplussed.

"Sure, Ian. I *have* been at this awhile."

Newcombe gave him a glance. But you haven't been with me, he thought.

"We'll be met by local officials. They don't know much about the project. They're just window dressing for your story."

"Got it. And the clones—will I be talking with them?"

"No. And try not to call them that in the story."

Harry was silent, mentally rummaging for a synonym.

They landed at the Kingdom's airport, soon being met by Troy and other police, along with Livia. The visitors were whisked past security checks and into a pair of police cars that sped off toward the capital and harbor. The occasional cyclist or peasant with farm animal was honked aside. Newcombe scowled at the clouds of dust and stench from huge mounds of garbage they passed. At a crossroads they passed a cluster of tacky businesses including the Big Gong restaurant, the gong on its sign flashing in the sun. This had better be worth it, Newcombe thought, but then he smiled. Window dressing, indeed. Harry would be taking his notes in the other car.

A police launch took the party to Progress Island, Newcombe's imposing size making him conspicuous to his welcomers. They were the same people who'd met David Pons, with the addition of the sergeant of the guards and an additional clone Robert had brought. There were no bags for them to carry, however, since this was a day trip. Ursula had brought a camera and duly recorded some handshakes and smiles to accompany Harry's story.

"But where's our guest of honor?" Newcombe asked Andrew.

"Mr. Pons? Seems he slept in today. But I'm sure he'll soon be about. He's a driven sort of person."

"Driven, hah? Well, let's get him driving in our direction."

As the group advanced to the compound, Livia walked with Troy and his junior officer. Carefully watching the people ahead of her, she tried to identify a helper for Cora's illness. Dr. Kenilwerth wasn't present and might be reluctant anyway. Livia needed someone with authority but not too long with the company. Dr. Shah seemed to defer to Andrew so, if she could just get Andrew alone, maybe . . .

But, on reaching the compound, they found David Pons having a late breakfast in the lunchroom. Unusually relaxed, he was content to bask in the convivial atmosphere afforded by Newcombe and his group. David could only convey positive impressions of the project, emotionally disinclined to argue or mount challenges. Ursula trained her camera again on the handshakes and smiles, Harry took easy notes, and the great meeting was quickly done with.

"Time to get the hell out," Newcombe muttered to Harry.

"We won't go around the island?"

"You can use some stock footage. We quit while we're ahead."

With some bemusement and trailing Newcombe's long strides, the group retraced its steps from compound back to police launch. As the other visitors were boarding, Livia laid a hand on Andrew's arm.

"I'd like to come back and see your new facilities, the education and rec centers, and see how they help the residents."

"Of course," said Andrew distractedly. "We're always available to you." Then, as if to be more friendly: "Maybe you can try the tennis courts!"

"Oh, do you play?"

"Well, I fool around a little with, ah, the residents."

"Okay. I'll be looking forward to it."

The launch pulled out and headed for the capital, a mood of accomplishment prevailing on board. Newcombe's impressive figure stood iconically above the waves.

———•———

Harry's report on the meeting, with supporting photographs by Ursula, spread quickly through the international media, chiefly in the business news. It was received with some surprise, since the very involvement of WHO had suggested some obstacles for the project. With the harmonious outcome, however, there appeared to be clear sailing for what could be a very profitable venture. This was especially appreciated by a group that had previously failed on Progress Island, causing them to meet in a special session.

A profound gloom filled the conference room, blinds fully closed against the bright sun outside. There was serious business at hand. This was a meeting of the Rumpers, a name assumed by the remaining investors–the "rump"–from the Vasquibo Institute, original underwriter of research on Progress Island. Most had quit the group, of course, following failure and liquidation, but these were the more stubborn of the colleagues. They'd believed there could be residual benefit, perhaps substantial, from their original bold commitment, and so they'd stayed together, pledging support for whatever opportunity might arise. The *de facto* head Rumper, seated at the head of the table, fully looked his part. Very broad and expensively suited, he sucked on a cigar that added to the room's opacity.

"So, Mr. Bernard," he said, "where do we stand on fulfilling our interests?"

The man he addressed, seated halfway down the table, was not a Rumper. He was Hugh Bernard, a partner in the law firm of Trotter, Bayes, and Wilke. The firm had been retained by Vasquibo during the promising first project, Bernard serving as lead counsel, and stayed with the Rumpers on an advisory basis. Bernard was tall and husky, with a high forehead, reddish hair, and faded freckles. His expression conveyed loyalty tempered by frankness.

"In terms of material gain," he said, "I don't see a successful action."

"Nothing on proprietary rights? Kenilwerth *was* our employee."

"Before you abandoned the project and later dumped the physical plant. No marketable process existed, that we know of anyway, and of course none is legally recorded."

"What about partial credit?" piped a Rumper down the table. "Can't we get a piece of the action based on it starting on our watch?"

"It *wasn't* started on your watch," Bernard responded. "The basic, flawed discovery was by Kenilwerth's husband, long deceased. It would be hard to show any progress at all while Vasquibo was running things."

There was silence, a billow of smoke from the head of the table.

"Surely," said the head Rumper, "we must have *some* option. We're alive, after all."

"I'm afraid I don't see a course."

Again the silence descended.

"What about—" began the man across from Bernard. "You have contacts, don't you? The firm, I mean. Special teams and that?"

"We use certain consultants occasionally," Bernard answered cautiously.

"No, I mean something more like action. Going outside the box."

Bernard eyed the man, perhaps the youngest member and normally a quiet listener.

"I don't know what you mean."

The head Rumper guffawed and slapped his palm on the table.

"Come on, Quentin! You started strong, let's hear what you've got. We need some movement on this!"

"Well, we've been talking about grabbing scraps, crumbs. Panhandling off Newcombe Ventures' success. But what if we were to make it *our* success, or at least threaten to? That might bring Newcombe to its knees."

"*His* knees, you mean?"

"No, the group. The big man's not in it alone. He can't stiff us without their consent."

"So, where's this success we threaten them with? They're the ones with the operation, the data, and soon the marketable process."

"But not yet. That's my point. Like Mr. Bernard says, nothing's been patented and such. The whole golden fleece is still up for grabs."

"You didn't answer the question, Quentin. Where's our leverage on this? We simply don't have any as far as I can see."

The young Rumper spread his hands, palms upward.

"We take it."

Hugh Bernard closed his portfolio, stared down at it with a grimace.

"You mean, *physically*?" someone asked.

"Yes."

"So, the talk of special teams was—"

Sabotage, Bernard thought to himself. Theft. He waited for objections, but none came. Instead there were neutral murmurs, a hint of interest.

"I don't like the way this is going," he said.

"Now wait a minute, Hugh," rejoined the head Rumper. "We have to get all options on the table here."

"Not with me around," and he rose and left the meeting.

A momentary silence followed the door closing. The head Rumper took a puff on his cigar as he surveyed his colleagues.

"Well," he said, "I guess we need a new lawyer."

———◆———

It had been cloudier than usual when they took the court, and it soon grew completely overcast. Livia was paired with Ursula for a friendly doubles match against Andrew and the clone known as Kittridge. Livia had improved her rudimentary skills while living in California, but the clone's aggressive game and matching demeanor distracted her. When the contest was reduced to Andrew trying to keep Kittridge friendly, the manager led the clone away and the two women played against each other. The air became less charged despite the overcast.

"Sorry about Kittridge," said Ursula. "He was the raw kind of clone, directly from a single genetic donor."

"You're working to, uh, socialize him?"

"Yes, and he's a candidate for aggression reduction. With gene therapy."

Livia paused, holding the ball.

"Can you go the other way on that? Someone's not aggressive enough, say a woman?"

Ursula stared at her, taken aback. Not her area, Livia thought.

"Kind of a finer point," Ursula smiled. "Might be down the road a bit." Then over her shoulder, taking up her position: "Andrew would know about it!"

Strange she didn't say the doctor, Livia mused, or the molecular biologist. But it was just as well. Andrew was the one she needed to reach.

When a light rain began they decided to call it a day. Andrew had returned and was standing by the entrance to the dining/recreation building. He suggested they have refreshments in the cafeteria, but Ursula said she had work to do so they should go ahead without her.

"But you'll get wet," said Andrew.

"I'll grab a shower at home," she said, edging away, then broke into a trot toward the compound, the old staff residence.

"She's very dedicated," Andrew informed Livia. "I couldn't ask for more in a financial consultant."

Livia could see they worked together closely and, given the situation—their being on the island and living in the same small building—were probably close personally as well. There was an edge of fondness to Andrew's professional praise, and warm deference toward him by a woman otherwise rather cool. Livia saw a need for discretion in exerting her personal charm, perhaps relying more on her official role, her authority.

They had coffee by a large window overlooking the southern shore. Large boulders could be seen dotting the water for some distance out. The continuing rain subdued the panorama.

"They had to clear a lot of brush here for the building," Andrew commented, "but it was worth it for the view. There's a salmon-colored sky after sunset, usually."

"Yes, it must be very nice," and Livia gazed into the rain. "I wanted to ask you about something though, Andrew. I mentioned it to Ursula but she said I should ask you."

Their eyes met and she waited a second, gaining his full attention, then described Cora's condition in as much detail as she could. Andrew listened patiently.

"She happens to be my niece," Livia concluded, "but also a citizen of the Kingdom, so I'm wondering on that basis if the project here can help her."

"Because of the agreement with your government?"

"Yes."

Andrew nodded thoughtfully, took a sip from his coffee.

"I hope I don't sound indiscreet," Livia continued. "I just thought it might be worked out. My sister, you see, the girl's mother, has been after me continually–"

"No, I understand," said Andrew, instinctively diplomatic. "As I understand it, though, the genetic basis of personality becomes very complicated when you're concerned with multiple traits. It's a lot bigger job than, say, curing Kittridge's aggression. It would likely have to be dealt with on a chromosomal level, a process Noelle–Dr. Kenilwerth–is working to perfect. I don't know how close she is exactly, I'll have to talk with her. But, even when she succeeds, the early applications will be considered experimental. I don't know if the parents, you know–"

"They're desperate, at least my sister. It's been going on so long."

Andrew paused, tried to see a larger picture.

"Whatever might be possible," he said, "there should probably be a non-relative involved in the request. We'd want it to be clear that it's all within the agreement, not something secretive that can get people in trouble. Or our company."

Livia nodded, averting her eyes to the rocky coastline in the rain outside. The handsome features of Troy Duillu appeared to her, suggesting him once again as the most promising contact for this.

5.

Several cars and a van from the Sydney police force were parked before a downtown office building. Everyone wanting to go in or out was subjected to search and questioning. Some of the elevators were not in service, still being examined for evidence of the overnight break-in and vandalism. The seventh floor was closed to all except authorized personnel. Here the headquarters of Newcombe Ventures, its outer offices defaced with spray paint, computers and other equipment tossed about, was presenting a challenge to local law enforcement. In the well-appointed but also trashed office of the CEO, Ian Newcombe stood conversing with the officer in charge.

"You'd no recent contact with the sort who are into this kind of thing?" the officer asked. "You know, rougher types?"

"Certainly not. We run a highly sophisticated business here."

"Well, it's clear you were singled out from the other firms in the building. There was nothing of much value, you say, among the items you noticed missing?"

"The wall decor was all prints, the vases and statues out of a kitsch catalog. There was no sane reason to break in and steal them."

"Which brings us back to the damage, sir, as if intimidation, perhaps revenge–but wait! What about information? Have you checked your records, files–paper *and* computer?"

"That would take some time, especially with the office in this state. Of course, most of what we do is public knowledge anyway. We're not a cloak-and-dagger operation."

"No, of course not. But it seems someone else is."

As the police work continued, a call came in on Newcombe's cell phone. Observing the caller's number, he knew that he should take the call. It was the same man who'd called him at the opera house to warn about David Pons. Sidling out of the room, Newcombe talked with his caller amid the hostile graffiti in the outer offices.

"Heard about your incident," the other man said. "Much damage?"

"Mostly just messy. We'll be back running in a day or two."

"Tap into the backup systems?"

"As needed, yes."

"They get anything I should know about?"

"Unknown. If so, it's in deep encryption."

"I'll be ready on the legal end. But you should know, if you don't already suspect, they might go after Progress Island next."

Newcombe hesitated, then: "So the game's afoot?"

"Afraid so. I was witness, actually, to the preliminaries."

"Aha!"

"You'll need to protect your interests, Ian. Physically. Sorry I can't help on that, but of course I'd risk exposure."

"I understand. But thanks for your other help, Hugh."

"Anything for an old schoolmate. Just about."

Livia rode in a tricycle to her lunch with Troy. The motorized three-wheelers were still the Kingdom's main taxi service. She could have called a government car, but they were meeting at Poseidon's restaurant, where she used to meet her husband before they were married. The tricycle was the best she could do then, so she took it today out of sentimentality. There was also a personal note, a hint of romance, that she planned to employ at this meeting, so arriving as she had before would prime her psychologically.

She put a hand to her hat as the tricycle whisked along. She was in the double seat behind the driver, a canopy above her. They left the city center and entered the commercial ring where it blended with the waterfront, eventually stopping before Poseidon's. Troy was sitting at a shaded table on the terrace, only having a soft drink since he was on duty. Livia alighted, regretful that she again had to barter her charms, yet committed to her purpose.

"You look beautiful today," he said, but he always complimented her.

"Did you have trouble getting away?" she asked.

"No, a quiet day. A cooler one, so quiet. Emotions simmer down, get mellow."

"Anything mellow on the menu?"

"Well, let's have a look."

She shouldn't have a drink, Livia decided, since Troy couldn't. This would hinder the kind of discussion she wanted to have, but it couldn't be helped. She therefore went right to the food menu to seek enrichment for their meeting. She selected an offering of prawns in glassy rice noodles with tiny blue eggs, while Troy ordered the local whitefish in sweet banyan sauce. Like Troy, Livia sipped calamansi juice as they waited for their food.

"So," Troy said, "you were back out at the project?"

"Yes, a little tennis playing. And some business, of course."

"Mm. A nice place to work, it seems. I get out there too, of course, but on the water. Not the same."

"It was nice going along with you that once. I enjoyed it."

Troy shrugged.

"Official business. We were both in our capacities."

Livia hesitated, tried to refocus.

"I talked with them awhile this time, the people in charge. Basically, on how their work will affect our society, our country. There's the agreement that we're to benefit."

"Yes," Troy nodded.

"It seems they're pretty far along in their research, including an area Dr. Kenilwerth specializes in. You know about her background?"

"Well, a little." He looked embarrassed. "I didn't have much science, you know."

"I didn't, either," Livia said quickly. "But they're discovering ways to help people with certain kinds of problems. In ways that weren't known or thought possible before. They can maybe help people with deep, ingrained personality problems."

Troy sat back, folded his arms.

"So, this might involve police work?"

"Well, I don't know. I was thinking more of people, of someone who's suffering personally, missing out on life because–"

She broke off. Neutral and unassuming, Troy waited for her to finish.

"For a citizen to be treated, of course, at least for now, the request would have to come from a government official."

Troy smiled.

"That would seem to be you or the Ministry of Health. Personally, I'd vote for you."

Livia smiled and weighed the thought, but of course it wasn't enough here. She'd have to describe the girl, not mentioning her relation at first, then gradually bring Troy in.

"Thank you," she said, "but I think it might depend on the type of case, and the circumstances. For instance—"

Troy's cell phone rang on his belt. He immediately answered it.

"Yes, Mr. Newcombe."

Troy quickly appeared concerned, then uncharacteristically severe.

"The nature of the threat, yes. If only we had a better time frame. But if your source is solid, yes, a response is necessary now. You can count on our commitment."

When the call concluded, Troy stood up from his chair and whistled loudly toward the inside of the restaurant. A second officer came running out, flicking aside a cigarette. Donning his cap, Troy gave Livia a hasty look of regret.

"Something's come up. Sorry."

And the two men were gone, jogging to their car parked down the street. Livia was alone in the pleasant shade, two unfinished drinks before her, thoughts and words involuntarily suspended. As the reality of the situation settled, the knowledge of having been thwarted, she also realized that she was relieved. She was still intact as a wife and professional, had not compromised herself. Somehow the wife identity seemed more important and she felt a flicker of yearning for California. Her loyalty to her niece and other family were still there, but how was she—one woman with one woman's life—supposed to gain what others wanted without losing too much herself? Cora could seek the treatment on her own later, or Mona on her behalf, when it was more proven and available. Or she could adjust to who she was in other ways. Aunt Xenia, after all, had never seemed all that unhappy.

"Will the gentleman be returning?"

It was the waiter, placing Livia's food before her, keeping Troy's on the tray.

"No, not today."

"I will package this for you?"

"Yes, thank you." And, smiling: "My dinner for tonight."

The waiter, who'd served her for many years, bowed and moved away.

On Progress Island, Noelle sat on a high stool in her lab, peering through a microscope at her successfully constructed chromosome. It appeared stable and was within size constraints imposed by a cell nucleus with full complement of natural chromosomes. She'd had to give up some life extension potential to allow for genetic material to help humanize the clones. This was consistent with research for human therapy, however, since some more complicated conditions might also require genetic space in the extra chromosome. There was the one Andrew had described to her, that sadly unmotivated girl in the Kingdom. And, closer to her own heart, there were people like Terence, so talented overall but destined for ruin by a tragic flaw.

David Pons came to mind, her surrogate Terence. But no, Noelle thought, she mustn't think that way. He was a man in his own right. His control on his obsessions was proof of that, set him apart from Terence.

"I'll be doing a follow-up report," David had spoken into the phone. "That's why I'm staying on here. I know I might have seemed, well, effusive early on, but my end product will be totally objective. It really is going well here, Dr. Shashemene."

He was over there now in the cottage, number 27, or perhaps strolling among the clones, curiously attempting conversation. Would he like to receive the chromosome someday, the version fully for life extension? Noelle couldn't foresee, but it didn't matter just now. She was happy with what had happened: they had met, it was going to last, it meant so much to them. True, he had to go back to Geneva. But her work here wasn't of indefinite duration. She'd reached a watershed, a basic goal of her involvement in the project. It was simply a matter of transition now, a well-charted course of briefing other personnel, turning her work over to them. Then she could follow David to Geneva, or they'd go somewhere else.

Outside, the day that passed on the island was typical. A wider, panoramic view, however, might have detected forces that could disrupt the progress of the Newcombe Ventures project. Defensive forces might also be sensed, creating an overarching tension to which most on the island were oblivious.

6.

Shots in the night.

David Pons sat up in bed, alert, trying to judge the distance. They were coming from various places, single shots at random intervals. Then some voices and rushing about.

"Do you hear that?" he asked, assuming Noelle was awake.

She raised herself on an elbow.

"It's happened before. Just stay in bed."

But David followed his instincts. Crouching in the dark, he moved to a window looking out on the cove. No sign of shooters, but people–more likely clones–were running hither-thither in a panic. A tall fellow came down the point, stopped when he neared the end, then crossed between cottages to the south coast. David went to another window to check on him, but the clone had disappeared. There was nothing visible on the sea from this point.

"David!" Noelle called. "Do come back!"

Turning away from the window, David did. The clone he'd been seeking, Kittridge, was in fact well along the south coast already. He'd shared in the panic of the others at first, but with running and getting away he was feeling much better. The beach was quite rocky here, so he moved inland a bit. Not too much since he feared the sharp sounds. He came to the stretch of boulders that extended into the sea like an archipelago. The dining/recreation building was off to his left. He'd just noticed a dim light on the sea, ahead to the east, when a man came running past the far end of the building, headed for the water. Kittridge instinctively headed for the boulders, seeking cover in their deep shadows. There was a sound of splashing as the man hastened into the water. There was the sound of a shot, then another that pinged off one of the boulders. Kittridge crouched in fear, a tight fetal position. The man's pursuers were running up to the shore. They stopped short of where the clone was hiding, talked in a language he didn't understand, first harshly and then calmly. Maybe about the light on the sea.

The men moved on, Kittridge sneaking a peek as they strode toward the cove. They were two of the guards who lived on the island's northeast corner. They'd see he'd run away, Kittridge thought. He sensed he'd better stay put, wait for the noise to stop, maybe for daylight.

"Be calm," Andrew always told him. "Just be calm." So that's what he'd do.

Andrew himself was huddled over his phone in the old staff residence, Ursula crouching beside him. He'd started for his office when the chaos started but retreated when he saw an intruder. Now he was talking with David Pons, trouble having spread to the cove, and he felt as pressured and powerless as he had once before in a leadership role.

"You're all right, then? You and Noelle are all right?"

"Yes, but what's this about? What's going on?"

"Just sit tight, David. The island's been—we have some intruders. The guards are engaged with them. We have to lock ourselves in, just hide. Help is on the way."

"Help from whom?"

"A police launch on patrol between here and the capital. They might be close by now. I was in touch with Lt. Col. Duillu. We had an alert during the day."

"One police boat? That's it?"

"He also has their naval and air wings standing by, but—well, I don't know how soon they can get here."

"How strong are they?"

"Three patrol boats and two light transport planes, I suppose with guns."

"What does our—what does the enemy have?"

"We know of two or three crafts and these operatives who came ashore."

"They just swam in from the sea?"

"On the eastern shore, yes. Least visibility. They might have been here awhile before the alarm went up. I saw one leaving our offices. We might not have seen them at all without the alert. Extra guards were out tonight."

"I see a couple of men now. Out there with the clones. They have their guns out. There's light from some of the houses, but I can't tell if they're guards."

"Keep your own lights off, David. And doors locked. We have to protect you and Noelle." He hesitated. "It could be Noelle they're *after*. Can you keep her hidden for us?"

"Yes, of course."

"Thank you. And good luck, David."

The police launch of which Andrew spoke had slowed on its approach to Progress Island. The officer in charge, Troy Duillu, had sighted lights on the sea to the east. He had the launch turn and cruise past the docking area. Gaining a better view, he counted two boats close to the eastern coast and another farther out to the southeast. There was also something small, a motorized dinghy perhaps, making its way to one of the boats. It was too far along to intercept without risk. Troy had no doubt there were weapons on the stationary craft. He decided to make a sweep past the island, giving notice of police presence, and hopefully dissuade any further aggression. After he'd completed the maneuver, however, Troy saw that the boats weren't moving, and there even came a sound of gunfire from one of them.

"Move back to the docks," he ordered.

"Will we be landing, sir?"

"After I make contact ashore."

But before calling Andrew he checked on the activity of the naval wing. Two of the patrol boats were en route, he was told, having been delayed by a problem with the third, which was apparently inoperable. Irritated and a bit worried, Troy contacted the air wing.

"Get those planes in the air immediately!"

A tense period followed, Troy electing to stay on the water and observe, judging this more productive than adding four officers to the land conflict. After about twenty minutes, the two patrol boats arrived, one making an aggressive sweep between Troy and the nearest enemy craft. The other shot around the island, taking position on the far side of the two threatening vessels. They were left a wide path to the open sea, an invitation to leave.

Time passed. The boats did not move.

Finally, on the police launch, Troy heard the hum of light transport planes. They approached from the west at high altitude, passed the island and circled back. One descended and flew over the island east to west, leveling off above the two hostile craft. Almost at once, perhaps before the plane came down, the craft were moving out. The two planes stayed in their patterns, the patrol boats stayed close to shore. Troy watched as the enemies slowly retreated, reached a distance equivalent to the third boat's off to the southeast, then stopped. Troy grimaced. It seemed he might have to attack, risk most of the Kingdom's defenses against unknown weaponry and skill. He forwarded a command to the lead transport plane.

"Try another low pass, gradual descent. No firing yet."

The maneuver was completed and the defenders watched expectantly. For a minute it appeared the boats were moving out, but they were simply separating themselves more. Troy was nonplussed at their recalcitrance, tried to gauge the risk of attack, imagine a strategy. The unknown factors and his limited forces again presented their conundrum.

"Sir," said an officer with binoculars, "off to the southeast. Third ship."

Troy took the binoculars from him and sighted as advised. The distant vessel had been joined by another form, moving irregularly around it. The new craft was in the air, a helicopter of military design, apparently harassing the boat below it. Flashes of gunfire were visible. The chopper withdrew and hovered some distance away, as if awaiting a response.

"The hostiles are withdrawing!" another officer called.

Troy turned to the two closer vessels. Sure enough, they were moving out to sea, accelerating strongly. So that was it, he thought, a command ship that held them here. The chopper: someone knew and went straight to command. But who? Who do we have to thank? He raised the binoculars again. The third ship was disappearing while the chopper moved closer to shore. Troy strained to examine it in the light of the quarter moon.

"Australian markings," he said to the officer nearest him.

The transport planes withdrew as the threat subsided, the patrol boats staying to guard the island. The helicopter made a studied approach and eventually came to rest on the little-used helipad. Troy called for another police boat to assist with any prisoners, then notified Andrew as the launch docked on the island. The police were met by several grateful guards, as well as a number of stunned clones. The land conflict had apparently dissipated.

Andrew had seen the helicopter approach and so, having heard from Troy, decided to emerge from hiding and survey the situation. Ursula was still at his side, as she'd been throughout the ordeal. Together they looked out toward the helipad.

"Shouldn't we check the offices?" she asked. "See what's missing?"

"You can if you want. I have to meet whoever's in the chopper. I'm still the manager here, supposedly in charge."

Ursula glanced back at the buildings, but took Andrew's arm. "We'll meet them together."

They walked through the field toward the chopper, on which the blades were slowing for lack of power. A door opened as the couple approached and a very tall, strong-looking man jumped out. He was followed by another, not as big but toting an automatic rifle. As the first man came into close view, Andrew and Ursula stared incredulously.

"Mr. Newcombe!" Andrew managed, as if to verify the sight.

"Yes," the CEO acknowledged. "Along with supporting cast."

Two more crew members had emerged and hung back with the rifleman.

"But how–" Andrew began, then simply spread his hands.

"Nothing unnatural about it, really. I'm still a reserve officer in our country. That and some personal pull, well–" He shrugged off further explanation.

"Well, thanks very much, Ian," said Ursula. "You saved the day."

Newcombe looked out levelly over the island.

"Group effort, Ursula. You held the fort till we arrived, along with our friends from the Kingdom. And that's what it's always going to take: people with intelligence and courage standing up against ignorance and evil. Against parasites like these tonight, itching to destroy or steal. Together we can stand against them, grind them into dust. Progress must go forward."

Newcombe's helicopter had been seen on its approach by Kittridge, who still lurked among the boulders on the southern shore. He'd also noticed its encounter with the third enemy craft, and the latter's subsequent departure. Now, with an air of calm descending on the island, the clone looked about and wondered what to do. He was without direction and, in his rudimentary mind, not without blame in this thing. He had run away, added to the problem, so he couldn't just go back and blend in. He had to do something else, something good, something that restored him to what he was before. But what had that been, exactly?

Kittridge rose from the boulders and saw the dining/recreation building. No one was about, the windows were dark. He cautiously circled the building to the entrance closest to the tennis courts. He knew this place and liked it; it gave him a good feeling. With a racket and some tennis balls he could play by himself till dawn, be like he was before, blend in. He stepped up and tried the doors but they were locked. They were heavy duty, just a foot-square window in each of them. Kittridge stared at them awhile, looked back at the empty courts, then slumped down against the doors, curling to one side. He'd wait here for Andrew, he decided. He could try some force but he'd get in more trouble, and he feared the force he'd witnessed this night.

I don't want that, he thought, and he slept.

To the west, on the southern point of Reverie Cove, David Pons had taken a call from Ursula and learned of the situation. Andrew and Mr. Newcombe were talking with Lt. Col. Duillu, establishing security now that the threat had been repulsed. The guards apparently had a prisoner and there were photos of the intruders' boats. There would no doubt be follow-up, but David should rest assured that the work on Progress Island would continue for the welfare of humanity.

"Well, it's over," he said to Noelle.

"Good," she replied calmly.

They were in the kitchen of number 27. They'd been sitting in the dark, but Noelle switched on the light over the stove.

"Shall we have some wine?" she asked.

"Why not?" David shrugged.

As they were sipping, Noelle glanced toward the door, each of the windows, the passage to the bedroom they were sharing, the bed.

"No matter how long we live," she said, "there are moments that live forever. In the ether, the upper reaches of all existence. Moments like tonight, the times of special significance. The trick is to avoid destruction, survive, and in good health. Then you can stay connected to the immortal moments and have their energy. You have it all to share with someone, someone attuned to you. We reinforce each other then. It's something even greater than immortality: a state of being that's beyond description, beyond imagination."

Though the small light was on, David thought he saw a glow in her features. The quarter moon was visible through a window. He nodded in response to her and sipped, the wine a decent Beaujolais.

From where she sat, Noelle saw now that he wasn't at all like Terence. And this was good, perfect in fact, because her life had run a purifying cycle. Her youth now was sublimely better than it had been the first time. The nascent tragedy in her love for Terence was absent here, she and the world gaining harmony with each other. A barrier of unreason had been passed to allow the rapid progress of humanity. A standard of perfection was at hand, the means to achieve it fast emerging, so a truly higher life form could now dominate the earth.

Paraprofessional

1.

Jobs were scarce during the recession, especially for someone my age. I was lucky enough to land a part-time spot at a rural mental health facility. As a counseling aide, I would mostly visit and talk casually with a list of residents. This gave the real professionals some relief, though it was theoretically for the benefit of the residents. If I heard anything important I was to inform my supervisor, Luverna. She and I were outside one day, discussing my list, when we noticed a female resident staring at us. The woman was short with wild gray hair, a small pale face with sharp features, and she had a wiry build.

"She looks excited," Luverna remarked. "Unusual for her."

"You're back!" the woman called over. "Back!"

"Yes," I said loud enough to carry. "Every Monday, Wednesday, and Friday."

The woman smiled, appearing delirious.

"That's Shirleen Doe," said Luverna. "We already had a Joan Doe and Joanna Doe in our files when she came. We named her Jolene Doe but she didn't like it. 'Make it *Shir*leen!' she said. So we did."

"You gonna talk to me?" Shirleen asked.

"He's just leaving," said Luverna. "Maybe next time."

We turned to go.

"*Will* you?" Shirleen demanded. "*Really?*"

I looked to Luverna, who nodded.

"Sure!" I called back, and we continued walking.

"What about the gender thing?" I asked.

All the residents on my list were male, in accordance with policy. Shirleen was no doubt on the list of a female counseling aide.

"We'll get an exception," Luverna answered. "Nobody's been able to get anywhere with her. I'll give one of your other cases to

153

Harry. Or I can assign Shirleen to myself, but you do the talking. Either way it's for her benefit. She's been like a clam in here."

"Okay," I said. "Glad to help."

Luverna gave an amused smile, perhaps thinking *that's what you're here for.* She was about ten years younger than me, a confident professional.

We continued into the building, I holding the door.

That was the first day.

Case Entry: Doe, Shirleen

Throughout our conversations, many of client's supposed memories are fragmentary and quite muddled. Little can be understood from them. Her earliest account with any coherence concerns walking down a street to buy a magazine.

As she walked, an occasional gust of wind would blow her hair back from her face. Shirleen would raise her shoulders then and shudder within her coat. The old houses seemed to be ignoring her. They were sullen, drained of their color under the stormy sky. The red ones seemed the saddest. Now and then, a leaf would flutter down in front of her. Why were they falling in spring? The trees were so scraggly, like they were sick. Still, they were something. Without them just narrow old houses pushing right up to the street.

She came to a corner drugstore. She'd bought popsicles here when she was little but they didn't sell them anymore. She entered and went to the magazine rack. The owner, an old man, used to get mad when kids would stand here reading the comic books.

"Do you have the June *Seventeen*?" she asked him.

"Not in yet. Should be in a couple days."

A bright cover caught her eye and she saw that it was *Time*. "The Hippie Phenomenon." Picking the magazine up, she found that the article was long. She'd have to buy it.

Outside, she tucked the magazine under her arm and walked down the business street. Small storefronts were soaped or papered over on the inside, *For Lease* signs taped against the glass. A small food store was closing for the day, the owner pulling a metal grate across the front, putting a padlock on.

Coming to another corner, she shielded her eyes from a whirl of dust. There was distant thunder and the county jail sprawled before her. Crossing over, she walked along the fence, gazing in at the massive structure. The wind played with her hair, making her squint with its gusts. There were prisoners inside, people locked up for doing something wrong, maybe hurting someone. But if they wanted to escape, was that wrong? It was if they meant to hurt someone, but just wanting to escape, by itself–who could blame them?

A car was honking across the street, a boy she knew asking if she wanted a ride. Shirleen shouted back, saying she'd walk, and the car sped off. Then she must have gone home.

A separate memory found her in her bedroom, reading for school. The clock ticked loudly and her eyes would stray once in a while to the other bed in the room. Its spread was white with little tufts and there was a pennant on the wall over it. Her sister was away at college, but it would only be for a year. Money was short.

Shouts came from the living room. Pa was watching the ball game with her brother and another guy. They were drinking beer.

Laying her book aside, she sat up on her bed.

It had been fun here once. That was when she was little, playing around the neighborhood and getting into trouble. But high school had been hard for her, and Ma and Pa watched her so close. Her brother, too. It was the movies or dance and come right home. That was the whole date. She might as well be going with another girl.

She got up to brush her hair. A friend of hers, another girl, was coming over soon. Shirleen had nice hair then, light brown with gold highlights, a little curly. She'd always been fair to pale, with hazy blue eyes. She sat straight as she brushed, petite but strong.

More shouts from the living room.

She found her friend in the kitchen talking to Ma, who had her worried little look. If only Shirleen could convince her that everything was all right, nothing bad was going to happen. They were just going for sodas and maybe to the other girl's house. Why was Ma so worried, looking up like that as she sewed up the holes in their socks?

"What time will you be in?"

"By ten, Ma, I think."

"Be careful now."

"Sure, Ma."

There was a screen door that slammed and wooden steps on which their feet must have been noisy. Here the memory faded.

Client also recalled a job she had in a dungeon-like factory, cartons of paperback books piled up to the ceiling. This was the warehouse she walked through on her way to the bindery. Other women in green work dresses moved slowly ahead of her, mostly in twos or threes. There were men too, laughing and swearing. Sometimes one of the huge brown bugs that lived in the cartons would run out into the aisle. Shirleen had thought they were mice at first.

She would stand on the line with seven or eight other women, a supply of book sections behind her. She would turn around, take a section from each pile, put them in order, turn around, and stuff the unbound book into the metal conveyor-rack. Then she'd do another one, and another and another, for eight hours not including lunch. When she was next to "A.B.," the friendliest of the other women, it wasn't so bad. They would talk and the shift would go by faster.

"When you going back to school, honey?"

"Just about a month, A.B."

"Think you'll miss this place?"

"I don't know. Maybe a little."

"No, you won't. You're too smart for that. Even I am. Even I'm too smart to like working at *this* place."

"Oh, A.B. I meant the people. You and a couple others."

"Sure wish *I* could go back to school. But I'm too old. Too old to go sitting in a classroom."

"No, you're not. There's lots of people *older* than you. They have special classes for adults and all."

"Hm. School's not what I need no how."

"Oh? What is it you need?"

"A rich old man who'll marry me then die. That's what *I* need!"

"A.B.!"

"That's right, honey. Someone I can just bury and have all his money so I won't ever be poor again."

They'd go on and on this way, packing book sections all the time. A.B. would occasionally ask Shirleen if she were ready for a break.

"I'm always ready."

"So am I. Too bad we have to wait for that man to turn the line off. He might as well go around with a whip, the way he works us."

"The men just walk off when they want."

"Mm. You're learning, honey."

Eventually, they'd touch on Shirleen's boyfriend, A.B. nodding toward a male coworker who grated on her.

"Your boyfriend's not like that–is he, honey?"

"Oh, no. He's nice."

"I hope so. But you got to be careful, honey. This here is a man's world. Don't you forget it."

Perhaps the coworker's emphasis helped strengthen this memory in client. No further details came through, however, about the job or her life at the time.

"I'm impressed," said Luverna. "What's your secret?"

We were at a table in the staff lounge, Luverna smoking.

"I can't say. She hits on something, I act interested. She says what she says."

"Good enough technique."

She tipped an ash from her cigarette, looking down at the metal ashtray. I noticed a concentration in her, a stillness to her sallow features, her loosely bunched brown hair.

"Have you thought about taking courses, Tom? Adding some credentials? If you have a knack–well, maybe there's a future here for you."

I laughed but caught myself. She was serious, after all.

"I'm kind of far along for that."

She looked at me for a moment, then shrugged.

"You never know."

She blew some smoke toward the vending machines, dismissing the subject.

"Now the boyfriend, she sort of skipped over him. Right? It'd be nice to know some more on that. Maybe you can steer her back that way."

"She's kind of rough steerage."

"Steerage. I haven't heard that word for a while. Well, if anyone can steer her you can. I'm glad I put you on her."

I felt a bit awkward and couldn't respond at first. After all, I was only there to make a few bucks till something better came up.

"I'll do all I can," I managed.

A woman came in to tap the coffee urn, cheerily greeting us on the way. Luverna gave a distracted wave.

"I wonder," she said. "Maybe I should pull another case from you. Or two, even. I want you to give Shirleen plenty of time."

Case Entry: Doe, Shirleen

Something with the boyfriend had happened during the summer, something nice Shirleen thought, and it affected her when she was back in school. The other girls, their activities, seemed too silly to her, as if they didn't know what was important, which was someone like Rick, or Nick, or maybe it was Rico or Stan. (To be called Rick in this narrative.) The school subjects, some of them at least, seemed more important to Shirleen since she needed them for college, for her and Rick's future.

He was in junior college but took little interest in his courses, it turned out. When Shirleen asked what subjects he was taking, he'd have trouble remembering. Their sole purpose was to keep him safe from the draft. He spent a lot of time at the campus, however, and much of his remaining time at work, pumping gas. Shirleen saw him less than ever.

"Rick," she said, "what do you do all the time at the campus?"

"Hang out. The lounge, the cafeteria, the gym."

"Who do you hang around with?"

"Guys from my classes. Friends. Whoever's around."

Guys. Always the guys. But inside, he wanted to be with her like during the summer. She was sure of it. He'd talked about a night at a motel, some time he wasn't pumping gas. It was okay that he didn't care about school, just so he cared about *her*. But what about the future? He didn't seem to care at all about that.

"Rick, do you think we might get married?"

"Huh?"

"If we keep going like we are now, do you think it'll end up that we get married?"

His response was to blow smoke hard and double up with laughter. When his breath was spent, he took a deep breath and laughed some more.

"Rick, don't."

She took his arm and squeezed it, but he couldn't control himself. That night, Shirleen went to bed rather puzzled.

Later, she apparently pressed for an explanation.

"Look," he said, "I like you. I like you a lot. But I don't go with you cause I want to marry you. Christ, why should I get married? I don't like kids, I don't have a good job–nada!"

"We could still get married if we want."

"But baby, I don't want to."

"Why do you go with me, then?"

"Like I say, I like you and–well, I figure I should put in time with you."

"What? Put in *time* with me?"

"Yeah."

"What do you mean? Why *put in time*?"

"Cause we been doing it."

Within herself, Shirleen began to hate the man–his appearance, his talk, his emotional distance from her. She suddenly hated everything about him. School was what counted now. Not all the silliness that went on, but the things that were interesting and made her think. It was important, of course, to have someone like Rick, to have a man. But his attitude and the hassle from her parents were too much. As winter set in, Shirleen would study hard and put Rick off when he called. She saw a girlfriend when she wanted company, though she realized it would never be good enough with another woman.

Client recalled another walk on her street, wondering why people didn't shovel their snow. The sidewalk was icy from packed down snow after many had walked on it. When it was windy then, or dark, it was easy to fall down.

There was no moon this night, only dim, dirty streetlights. The snow was all dirty and crusty, the flat-faced stone houses looking very cold, adamant: You are not welcome. There was no one on the streets, the cold keeping them in. Too cold for robbers and jerks, Shirleen thought. Stay in and keep warm, make trouble when it's nice out. More lights ahead, the business street. Why am I out here walking? The cold, the pain of winter–feels good when you go in. Light at the end of the tunnel. All emptiness now but, somehow, there's hope.

She passed an old lady holding a shawl over her head, shivering, picking her way along the ice.

She was like me once. Time and weather, the cold. And hard work and sadness. Life isn't just hard. It can be brutal to some people. A conscious, deliberate force that hits them again and again until they submit, until they are broken. And when they are miserable, they just stay that way. Until they die and everybody forgets about them.

She passed a tavern that was still open. The beer smell came through even though the tavern was shut tight against the cold. County Jail was across the street, also shut tight.

Oh, that wind! So freezing in the darkness, so much worse than when there's light. Sweeping down from the Arctic, across Canada. Is winter nicer in the country? It always looks so nice on Christmas cards.

Shirleen became silent in her reverie but was smiling. She perhaps was dwelling on inexpressible thoughts.

2.

A miniature fountain trickled on Luverna's desk, filling the gaps in my reporting on my clients. Neither of us liked to meet in her office, myself especially. It gave me a bad feeling from my past, my being called on the carpet in other places. She had reports to finish for the administrator, though, so we hadn't much choice today.

"Harry was good about another transfer from you," Luverna commented. "Josie bristled a little with hers, got into the gender policy and all. But we'd already crossed that line when I gave you Shirleen. And she's a priority now, pure and simple."

"It's all okay with Mrs. Arnold?" I asked, referring to the administrator.

Luverna kept her eyes on her papers.

"So far, so good," she answered.

I saw my supervisor as efficient, methodically clinical, but with some kind of underlying impatience. She had a distaste for mundane details and would skip over them if she could get away with it. This tendency could propel her further into testing limits.

"Actually, I'd like to let a student handle those cases, but there's those state guidelines. Paid staff only, accountability."

She spoke with something like sarcasm. Clearly enough, she chafed under restraints even while working diligently. I felt some desire to help her.

"Maybe you could have a student help with your reports," I suggested. "That would free you up for other things."

She looked up with a surprised smile.

"Confidentiality, Tom. But thanks for your sympathy."

The little fountain trickled close to where I sat. It was the only noise for a moment as I returned her look, the new feeling beneath our formal roles. She shared the quiet office with another supervisor who wasn't there but could return at any time.

"You know," Luverna said, "with the complications arising in Shirleen's story, we might do better to discuss her off-campus. Give it our undistracted attention. Next time maybe, if that's all right with you."

"Sure, I'd be happy to."

"Good."

We got back to work then, but I had the sense we'd moved to a new phase in relation to each other, something beyond our obligations to Shirleen and others at the facility. Yet Shirleen was the catalyst, or rather her case, her condition was. If this went anywhere with Luverna and me, we'd more or less owe it to Shirleen.

Case Entry: Doe, Shirleen

Client has had memories of attending college, or rather, scenes and incidents of that period in her life. She apparently commuted to an urban campus. Of the college itself, she recalled sitting in an outdoor amphitheater, other students also sitting or sprawling on the stone steps. Autumn sun was flooding in, creating a glare, but her sunglasses protected her.

"Che! Che! Che!"

A dozen or so demonstrators with signs marched into the space below. Students looked up noncommittally from their books or conversations.

"Che Guevara lives forever in the collective conscience of the masses!"

The leader's words reverberated over the stone steps and his companions cheered. Shirleen watched them, detached, recalling the news photo of the slain revolutionary. Finality, she thought, there's no denying it. Dead is dead.

Shirleen enjoyed being in college. She'd always sit near the front of the lecture hall since people were talking and fooling around farther back. When there was a test, she had no trouble applying herself to studying. When she was only reading or preparing a written assignment, however, her mind would often wander.

Almost every day she found herself idling somewhere on the campus. She'd sit in one of the cafeterias, or in a lounge, or somewhere outside, and read or pretend to read or simply do nothing. She was waiting, really. Not for someone from one of her classes. They would simply talk about the class. Nor for someone she'd known in high school. She was waiting for someone new, someone who was interesting and fun and who'd introduce her to people and activities that would make her life full and important. She'd taken up smoking and felt secure and sophisticated as she sat and waited amidst the fading wisps of her cigarette.

Sometimes, rather than simply idle, Shirleen found little activities to attend. She took in the experimental films that were shown for free, sitting by herself in the dark of the viewing room. Few people attended these films except for one which showed hippies copulating in a pig sty. Shirleen also went to hear the guest speakers, many of whom were radical. She only had to pay once, when Dr. Leary came. The huge room was packed as he spoke against the war and antagonists of the drug culture. His wife sat beside him holding a huge flower, and it occurred to Shirleen that this woman was only a few years older than herself.

It was easy to know what there was to do. Bulletin boards were everywhere, announcements seeming to fight each other for space. Shirleen would often examine them, even in the rain, as other students hurried by. By the end of the quarter, she was very curious about the short, strongly worded messages from the S.D.S. and other groups of radicals.

———·◦·———

Client recalled an incident from a job she held during Christmas season, apparently during that first year of college for her. It was behind a counter at a downtown department store. Her feet would hurt after a few hours and she'd be bored and restless. She'd watch the shoppers rushing along, eager to spend money, and think of the dollar thirty-five an hour she was being paid. It somehow didn't make sense to her, didn't seem fair. The experience was uninteresting and painful and the rewards for her pain weren't enough. Things just didn't balance out.

"Do you have this in a fuchsia?"

"What?"

The older woman smiled in condescension.

"Fuchsia, my dear. It's a color–light, bright reddish purple."

"Let me check."

Shirleen opened the cabinet below the counter and brought out some cashmere sweaters.

"We don't seem to have one in exactly that color. Here's one in a rose color. Is that close enough?"

"No, my dear, I'm afraid not. Rose is simply not fuchsia. Here, let me see those."

Shirleen watched the aged hands picking through the sweaters, the delicate gold watch with little diamonds, the rings with stones that just couldn't be real, she thought.

"Tell me, what do you charge for seconds in this item?"

"All our seconds are sold at half price."

The shopper pulled a light blue sweater out of the stack.

"Here. Look at this."

"What?"

"Can't you see? This sweater is soiled."

"It is? Where?"

"Look. See, right here."

The woman waved her finger toward the neckline. Shirleen looked closely but couldn't see what the woman was talking about.

"I'm afraid I don't see anything. Maybe it's the light."

"Nonsense. This sweater is soiled and should be sold as a second."

Shirleen hesitated. What was this old lady trying to do?

"No, ma'am. The price is $39.95."

"I insist you sell it to me at half price!"

"No, ma'am. I can't do that."

"You'll do it or I'll see the manager and have you fired!"

Some people looked over and a wave of embarrassment warmed Shirleen. What a bitch this woman was! Why didn't she just wipe herself with it? Then it would really be dirty!

"Well, are you going to ring it up?"

Shirleen laughed in her face.

"What! We'll see about this!"

She flung the sweater away and bustled off, shooting back several grimaces. Shirleen refolded the sweater and put it away with the others. Thinking on what had happened, she didn't feel bad. She'd been spontaneous, yet she'd been right. Cut through the complications, she thought, like the radicals at school. They're right sometimes but they act kind of crazy so people don't listen.

The holiday season was windy and snowless and Shirleen was eager to get back to school. The decorations reminded her of her job in the department store, and she didn't feel as close to her family as before. She felt lonely on New Year's Eve, wishing she was in a snow-covered cabin, snuggled close to someone in front of the fireplace. Someone strong, gentle, intelligent. Someone who had ideas like a radical but was respected by people and not aggressive.

———•———

With the winter quarter came snow and bitter cold. Jeeps were plowing snow all over the campus, and the central amphitheater was just a big white bowl with an icy path through its center. Over this path students rushed from the library to the Student Union and vice versa.

Once in a while, since she couldn't sit outside, Shirleen would sit in the Student Union's TV rooms, where a set in each room was continuously tuned to a single station. She'd still check all the bulletin boards, though, for more interesting things. One afternoon, when it was already getting dark, she saw a young man in hooded jacket tacking up announcements. It was very cold but he seemed unhurried as he tapped with a small hammer. Passing behind him, Shirleen stopped to view the announcement. The young man turned and smiled at her.

"It's a McCarthy rally. They'll be organizing volunteers for the Wisconsin primary."

Shirleen took a half-step sideways, about to walk on, but there was something in his easy movements, his speech, and his eyes that she couldn't walk away from.

"Will there be peace movement speakers?"

"Sure, people from lots of different groups. McCarthy's campaign manager will be there to handle the recruitment."

"Will you be there?"

What made her say that? Before she could become embarrassed, however, the young man smiled and put her at ease.

"Of course. Why don't you come? I'll introduce you to some of the peace movement people if you like."

"Okay." And she smiled back at him.

Although his hood was up, she could see his hair was dark blond and longish. Some fell over his forehead and more stuck out along the sides. She couldn't see what color his eyes were; they were set deep and the sun had gone down.

"By the way, my name is Jim."

Although he might have said Tim, Shirleen thinks now, or even Jack. But we decided to stay with Jim for our conversations.

"I'm Shirleen."

"You look cold."

"Yes. Guess I'll go to the Union and warm up."

He said he'd see her later, at the Union or at the rally. Shirleen isn't sure which it was, just that it seemed colder than ever when she was away from him.

———◦———

"You're getting a lot from her," Luverna commented. "A pretty decent history. And interesting. I can sense the period."

We were in her apartment, close to the facility but beyond its control. We sat on opposite ends of a couch, tubular steel and black leather. There were abstract paintings on the walls, as well as primitive masks, and carved wooden figures of animals on tables and shelves.

"She can really come out with the details once she gets going," I said.

Luverna nodded over the folder, cigarette in hand.

"So now we have Jim, not Rick. Rick's out of the picture."

"So it seems. For now, anyway."

"Yeah, we don't know where she's going to take us. Maybe she doesn't, either. We don't know how much of this even happened, after all. Right?"

I nodded my assent.

"I was wondering," I ventured, "if we were going to involve Dr. Greenberg soon."

The facility was occasionally visited by a consulting psychiatrist, our state's budget not permitting one on the permanent staff.

"No," Luverna said absently, "later." She studied the folder. "This is a little before my time, but–" A coy smile. "Not yours, right?"

"Yep, I'm about that vintage."

Her smile widened.

"But a little sweeter variety, I'd say."

I was stuck for a response. She was my supervisor. Yet, curled on the couch without a therapist coat, she looked quite appealing to me.

"Actually, I have some around. You've given me a taste now. Have a glass with me? No guarantees, but I sort of like it."

"Well, I have the drive."

I was living in another town, traveling to and from the facility past rural plains. But Luverna just kept looking at me, waiting for me to say more.

"I guess just one would be okay."

She flipped on the sound system on her way to the kitchen. Subdued band music floated through the living room. I looked toward the patio door, the failing light outside. I considered switching on a lamp, but Luverna was returning already with glasses of wine.

"So," she said, "you're really into Shirleen's life. It's amazing after all the months of stonewalling we got."

I shrugged.

"I'm as surprised as you are."

"And you never did this before, got someone to open up like this, as a counselor of some sort?"

"Not really. I was just a case manager–financial, medical, making referrals to people like you who knew what they were doing."

She held up two fingers crossed.

"Let's hope so."

"Well, I mean probably."

"Yes, probability. Good as anything to live by. Right?"

"I suppose."

She'd made no move to put on a light, was sitting a cushion closer to me on the couch. I sipped my wine, leaving the ball in her court. Experience dictates discretion.

"Want to dance?" she asked.

What else could I do? I lowered my glass to the coffee table as she drank deeply from hers. She led me to an area before the patio door lit by the remnants of sunset. The band played on from the sound system hidden in shadows.

Case Entry: Doe, Shirleen

It might have been after the rally, or maybe another time, but client recalled walking through slush with Jim and another male, Jim's friend. They were talking about whether or not to attend a certain concert. They reached Jim's car and he dropped off the friend, then turned to Shirleen sitting beside him.

"Like to stop by the Monk's Cell?"

"What's that?"

"My apartment."

"Why do you call it a monk's cell?"

"Because it's very small," he smiled, "and very humble."

They drove only a few minutes and then turned into a quiet

side street where Jim parked. Shirleen followed him to a two-story cottage behind an old stone house. They climbed an outside staircase to the second floor, where Shirleen waited as Jim searched for a light switch inside.

"Does anyone live downstairs?" She asked.

"Yes, a restaurant worker. Nice guy."

The room was lit by a dim, unshaded bulb. There was an old stove next to a sink and a large metal box, painted black.

"What's that?" Shirleen asked.

"My refrigerator."

"Why is it black?"

"I don't know. It was like that when I moved in."

The apartment was just one big room with a sort of bathroom closet added. There was a mattress on the floor and an old, scarred desk with a lamp on it. Books and art materials were scattered about and there were masks and posters on the walls. Jim gestured toward cushions on the floor and Shirleen sat down.

"Like some fruit juice? I have tea, but I know you drink coffee."

"What kind of juice is it?"

"Kumquat."

"Are you serious?"

He poured two small glasses from a pitcher in the black refrigerator. Handing one to Shirleen, he sat in front of her and proposed a toast.

"To peace."

"Yes, to peace."

They drank.

"Are you really a radical?" Shirleen asked.

He looked to one side and seemed to concentrate. When they were in quiet, dimly lit places, his eyes appeared so deep beneath his mane of hair that Shirleen saw him as a lion.

"In my political beliefs, in my attitude toward society, I guess I am. But in my personal values, my ideas on lifestyle, there are probably a lot of people who feel the same way and don't seem radical at all. I'm basically a very simple man, Shirleen."

He hesitated a moment, then continued.

"I feel the need to support radical causes, to work actively for them, because we live in the shadow of tyranny. It's the same in other countries. As long as the present pattern exists, this state of everyone being at the mercy of a few politicians, generals, and millionaires, there has to be some resistance. Otherwise, it means we accept their total power, no matter how unfair or arbitrary their decisions."

"Do you think the radicals can win?"

"In our country, probably not. It doesn't seem possible. But we can influence the power brokers' decisions on individual issues. Like right now there's the war."

"I like the way you describe things, Jim. It makes me understand them better."

"Thanks, but I don't really have any answers. I can only support movements that seem to be in the right direction."

Shirleen glanced around the room.

"How long have you been living on your own?" she asked.

"A couple years. Since high school. I moved in here in the fall."

"It must be nice–not having anyone to answer to, just coming and going as you please. And you can study without any distractions. I like the way you live. You're so free!"

Jim smiled and leaned toward her.

"Yes. But you know, Shirleen, quite often I feel lonely. So I tend to go out a lot."

"It's funny, Jim. I like to go out, too, but not because I'm lonely. It's more to get away from the people at home. I don't feel free with them. I feel closed in. I feel like I'm being forced to live their way, to believe what they believe."

"Most parents, I think, will only treat their children as adults after they have children of their own."

"But that's not right."

"No. But it isn't important, either."

She studied his face, his confident smile, and felt a decision rising.

"I like you, Jim. I like you a lot."

"I like you too, Shirleen."

She toyed with the small glass that had held her kumquat juice, waiting out the emotion that was rippling through her. Jim studied her hand, her blue eyes, her brown and gold hair, curly near the ends.

"Want to stay?"

Shirleen nodded.

She awoke in the monk's cell next morning as winter sunlight filtered through the room. Against her heart she held Jim's sleeping head and twined his tawny hair around her fingers. She could feel the warmth of his body in the chill morning, and the warmth of her own.

This was peace.

3.

The bedroom was dark except for outside light filtering in. It was brighter than it would usually be due to fresh snowfall, still in progress. Luverna lay beside me, turned away on her side, breathing quietly. I myself hadn't slept yet. She'd wanted to dance again on this visit, but this time it led to something more, a lot more. The wine, our growing familiarity, and that certain anxiety in her, that need, opened the way to here, her bed.

Looking at her dim form, I wondered where this might lead. What was possible for us? Like me, Luverna apparently had a rocky past in her relationships, though I didn't have many details on them.

"He flipped out," she'd said of her ex-husband.

"What do you mean? How?"

"That's *it*. He just flipped out."

There was also the place we worked, the facility. Anything between staff members was noticed, talked about, and Luverna was my supervisor. The administrator, Mrs. Arnold, had a friendly, folksy way about her, but I was wary of an underlying rigidity so common in these semi-rural areas. She wouldn't be in her position if she didn't share in it.

I leaned over to touch Luverna's shoulder.

"I'm awake," she said.

"I guess I am, too. Not dreaming, I mean."

She turned over so she faced me, raising herself on an elbow.

"Having second thoughts?" she asked.

"About what?"

She laughed.

"Maybe you're thinking about another go-around."

"Well, the snow's pretty deep by now, I think."

She relaxed back onto the pillow.

"Yes, we have all night."

172

"Actually," I said, "I was thinking about you. How you were early on, just out of school and getting into your chosen work."

"Hm, yes. Full of enthusiasm, professional zeal. Then, not too far along–"

"Hit a wall? Disappointment?"

"More like stagnation, with an occasional sense of purposelessness."

"But, the humanitarian thing, helping people. Isn't that what drove you, starting out?"

"Ah, those telltale words, 'starting out.' Before you know how entrenched everything is–the institutions, attitudes, financial and legal constraints, et cetera, et cetera. And knowing that, in the end, you're not going to make a damn bit of difference in the parade of pathetic creatures who come at you. Knowing you're just part of the official B.S."

I hesitated. I'd had this conversation before, at other times, other places.

"A crappy system, yeah. Most systems are. But if it's all you have to work with, what can you do? Just your best, right? And no regrets."

"You believe that, Tom?"

"Well, I'm able to. It's an available response."

She was silent for a moment.

"Would you like to move in here?" she asked. And, when I didn't respond: "It'd be handy for snowstorms."

We both laughed.

"There's that difference that's there," I said, "between visits and all the time. A good relationship can be ruined by it. I think often it's inevitable."

"Speaking from experience?"

"Yes, though of course things get spoiled in other ways, too."

"How true. But then, if that weren't the case we wouldn't have much business."

And we wouldn't have met, I thought, wouldn't be meeting here to discuss a special case. I reached over to touch her and she caught my hand, pulled me toward her. The sound of a passing snowplow marked the end of our conversation.

Case Entry: Doe, Shirleen

Client recalled that, through the placement office at college, she'd gotten a summer job as a day camp counselor. There were jobs that paid more, but factories and stores and such were part of her past now. She was escaping from the treadmill.

As a counselor, she'd take the children places or teach them things and feel as important to them as a mother. She could be firm when necessary and was pleased when a child responded to her correction. But her main satisfaction was that, for a few hours a day for a few months, these children needed her. Her meeting their needs added meaning to her existence.

"Jim," she said, "I think I want to major in something where I can work with people. Helping them, I mean. I like the feeling it gives me."

"Well, there's teaching, social work. Nursing, too, but that takes a lot of science."

"How about if I major in psychology?"

"Yeah, you could be a counselor, social worker, something like that. Maybe pretty high-paying if you go to grad school."

She looked at him in the dim light of the monk's cell. Sounds of the city at night could be heard through the open windows.

"You don't really care about all that–do you, Jim?"

"About all what?"

"Grad school, careers, and all."

"Well, no. I guess not. Working with people itself is different, though. I might get into it myself, in some way."

She lay back and looked at him. He'd been unusually quiet this night.

"What do you think about when you're so quiet?"

"Oh, sad thoughts mostly. About time, how hard it is to hang on to something good, once you find it."

"Do you have something good now?"

He leaned over and kissed her.

"So do I, Jim. But don't ever think about losing it."

"I can't help it, Shirleen. I got a letter from the draft board today. They reclassified me."

"Took away your deferment?"

"Right. Oh, I won't get drafted tomorrow. Sooner or later, though–"

They were silent a moment.

"Will you go, Jim?"

"No, of course not."

She took him in her arms and laid her head on his chest.

"Let's not worry about it tonight. Maybe you can just get it changed."

He laughed a bit and caressed her hair.

"Okay, no more of that tonight."

———◦———

Client's memories of the convention riots were fragmentary and disordered, difficult to elucidate. She was apparently living away from her family at the time, presumably with Jim. Many activists were pouring in from out of town. They camped in a large park area, living a freewheeling lifestyle. Their plans for the convention were often preparations for conflict, and there were preliminary skirmishes with police. There was much drug abuse, arrests, rising anger and resentment of authority.

There was a march downtown, where the radicals were to join with more moderate groups and march on the convention center. There was conflict with police along the way, with much shouting and defiance, objects thrown, beatings, tear gas, running and regrouping. Most of the radicals, Shirleen and her friends among them, reached the point of convergence with the other demonstrators. On trying to approach the convention, however, they were confronted by phalanxes of blue-helmeted police.

Shirleen recalled a voice on a bullhorn, a token warning perhaps, and blue lights flashing everywhere. Then the police charged in with Mace and flailing clubs. The beating went on and on, Shirleen scrambling to get away past fallen bodies. There was a chant that rose from the periphery, a chant that the whole world was watching. Then all went blank.

—— · ◆ · ——

Sometime after the convention, Shirleen and Jim walked through drizzle near a city train station. He looked straight ahead as he walked, she down at the sidewalk, at the cracks.

"I want to go with you," she said.

"It wouldn't be good just now. I have to find a place and get myself together. And you need to stay in school."

"I need to be with you, Jim. Don't you see?"

He bit his lip and heaved one of his knapsacks into a more secure position.

"Yeah, I see."

She looked at him as they stood at the last stoplight before the train station. So good and great he was, yet pushed around and beaten by slobs, hate-filled weaklings. Now he was forced into exile because he wouldn't do their dirty work, their killing and blowing up. Forced away from his friends and places he knew, forced away from her, and she from him.

"I'm sorry, Jim. I'm making it harder for you. You're right, of course. I should stay in school and go later. We'll live together just like we did here. Won't we?"

"Sure. Of course."

They entered the huge station and took an escalator down to the old waiting room with its massive benches. She stood with him as he waited to buy his ticket.

"Damn it, Shirleen. I'm sorry."

"No, that's all right. I'll be okay."

He kissed her.

"I'll write and call you, and you'll be coming up later."

They forced smiles and hugged each other.

"I like that, Jim. I'll think about it all the time."

But she cried in the departure area, thinking again about the unfairness of it all. She collapsed into his arms and sobbed against his coat. It was always this way, she thought. As soon as you found something good–happiness or a way to help people–complications set in and suffocated, strangled, shut off the life–the promise–of all that you had. The world seemed just one big bureaucracy controlled by ruthless, invisible sadists.

"I have to go now, Shirleen. The train leaves in a few minutes."

They kissed and he picked up his bags. Out on the concrete pier, they embraced again as he boarded the train. Then he swung his knapsacks up and leaned over from the steps.

"Good-bye, and peace."

"Yes, peace."

And they kissed for the last time.

Client recalled studying a great deal, letting her mind be stimulated and new curiosity fill the void left by Jim's departure. She wanted to absorb what she studied and become more, grow intellectually. She believed there was power to be gained from knowledge, power that would enable her to control her own life, achieve what she needed. She sought to escape forever the swamp of mediocrity that had held her captive.

The very language of psychology, Shirleen's major, came to attract her. She enjoyed thinking of behavior in terms of motivation and levels of consciousness, or personality in terms of hereditary versus environmental factors. She'd build up her knowledge of psychology and deepen her understanding of people until they could no longer hurt her.

Besides the knowledge, there was the simple thrill of functioning intellectually. Her mind was becoming tuned, exercised, so it could make correct decisions based on her growing store of knowledge. She was no longer just her physical self. She was a mind, someone whose opinions were informed, who could converse with other intellectuals on important matters. It was partly because of Jim and partly because he left her. Because, after he left, she had to study so much to escape the pain.

———•———

One day the following year, as Shirleen was walking through a chilly drizzle, the answer to everything came very suddenly. She was on the edge of the city, in an upscale neighborhood on the lake, and she shivered within her coat. She'd been feeling stressed from her studies and used some pills she'd been given, but they sometimes had bad effects. She needed something else. As she looked up at the sky, gray but not dark, it suddenly seemed that there was great meaning. Everything was as it should be and good because things were as they were by the hand of Someone or Something greater than everybody. She felt such an abundance of meaning and human goodness in her that it lit the entire street, gave it life.

There was a church in the distance. Shirleen felt drawn to it.

As she approached, she noticed a door propped open and many cars parked outside. It was Sunday morning. Standing before the sign, she read the denomination, different from her own. No matter; a church was a church. They all seemed holy.

Once inside, she hesitated. The minister was standing at a podium in front, reading a report of some kind. An old man sitting on the aisle turned around and scrutinized her. A younger man sitting next to him pulled on his arm and urged him to pay attention. Pushing back her damp hair, Shirleen stepped forward. Ignoring the congregation, she walked directly toward the front of the church and the minister. He stopped speaking as she drew near, returning her gaze in silence until she halted in front of him.

"Good morning, sister. The usher will show you to a seat."

A man approached from one side but, before he could take Shirleen's arm, she dropped to her knees.

"Behold the handmaid of the Lord!"

The minister and his usher looked at each other dumbly, then back at Shirleen.

"Behold the handmaid of the Lord!"

Her cry mesmerized all present. She was holding out her arms in supplication. The usher was powerless but the minister recovered and beckoned to his wife in the front row. She got up and came forward.

"I'm the mother of God!" Shirleen shouted. "I'm having your baby! Your spirit is filling me and bursting out! Light of the world! I'm the holy virgin!"

"Hallelujah!" someone shouted. It was the old man. "She's saved! Hallelujah!"

He was jumping up and down, people trying to restrain him. At the front, the minister's wife talked cajolingly to Shirleen.

"Sister, come with me. Pastor will talk to you after the service. Come with me, now. I want to help you. Come."

Shirleen looked at her blankly, then struck out with clawed hand and left four red streaks across the woman's face.

"Shut up with your crap! I'm the light of the world!"

"Hallelujah!" the old man shouted. "Praise God she's saved!"

The minister came from behind the podium and stood in front of Shirleen. She looked at him and spoke imploringly.

"I'm the mother of God! I'm having your baby! Take me into your house and make love to me!"

The minister's wife was sobbing on the floor, holding the wounds on her face. The usher, totally confused, looked desperately to the minister.

"Get the police," he was told.

4.

The restaurant had plenty of candles but not much other light. Luverna and I had held off ordering dinner, wanting to talk awhile over cocktails. She was tenser than usual, smoking, gazing into open spaces of the restaurant. Mrs. Arnold was across the room with her husband and another couple, well into their meal. Luverna had acknowledged her superior with a brief wave but otherwise avoided eye contact. Her only comment on the situation had been "Oh, no!" when she first noticed it. I'd taken a quick glance.

"We'll have to bring Greenberg in on Shirleen," Luverna said.

"It's gone that far?"

"Yeah, you're into his territory. Then there's her." A head jerk toward Mrs. Arnold. "She'll be reading the file now."

"She'll involve herself with the case?"

"I hope not. Not too much, anyway. We want it to cover *this*, with us."

I nodded along but sensed a problem developing.

"Look, if a change becomes needed, I'm just part-time. I can find something else. There's no need for you to have to deal with it."

Luverna frowned, flicked ash from her cigarette.

"No, no change. We have Shirleen's case. For that bitch over there that's all this is."

"Right," I responded, refraining from further suggestions. Like Luverna, I really didn't want any kind of change for us.

"Guess it's good you didn't move in," she said. "They'd have us dead to rights."

I laughed. Luverna didn't.

"I'll get copies of your reports to Greenberg," she continued, "arrange for a meeting on Shirleen during his next visit."

"Any way I can help?"

"Just talk with Shirleen, then have the new material ready for the meeting." A hesitation. "I mean, if you were asking professionally."

I glanced again toward Mrs. Arnold.

"Guess that's all I better do here."

Luverna finally smiled.

"They'll be leaving before us. Then we'll do what we want, *where* we want."

"Consenting adults."

"Of sound mind."

The restaurant patter continued around us. We eventually had dinner, then drove past rural plains to my place in another town. The thought of Mrs. Arnold's scrutiny kept us from Luverna's that night.

Case Entry: Doe, Shirleen

Client had little recall of the period following her breakdown, but she apparently resumed her studies and managed to graduate, eventually finding employment as a school counselor in a rural community. She rented a room on the edge of town and bought an old used car to drive to work. She liked her job and people respected her, but there was something very wrong for her. When she came home to the big house full of rented rooms, there was nothing there for her, no one who cared about her professional status. She was intensely alone in the long rural nights. She didn't want a relationship, afraid from the past of what might happen, but there was still that gnawing need within her. Of necessity, then, her work came to be everything for her. She *was* her work. She'd be defensive if anyone disagreed with her because they threatened her existence.

The last student she counseled, who might have been named Randy, had been suspended for misconduct on the school bus. Another boy had written a word on Randy's hand and given him a nickel to show the word to the bus driver.

"Do you know what that word means?" Shirleen asked.

"No, ma'am. If I knew it was a bad word, I wouldn't have done it. Honest."

She looked at the suspension notice: extremely immoral behavior, indefinite suspension. It was signed by the grade school principal, recalled as "Mr. Smetters."

"How long do I have to stay home, ma'am? I'm not too good at arithmetic and I might flunk if I miss too much."

"I don't know, Randy. I have to talk with your parents and get back to Mr. Smetters. We'll get you back soon as we can. Okay?"

She smiled but Randy didn't. He was worried, didn't want to flunk.

"Are we friends, Randy?"

"Yes, ma'am."

The parents were quite passive, Shirleen found, submissive to the will of the school. She was thus alone in her efforts to persuade the principal. Her previous contacts with him had been brief and formal, no real issues having arisen during her month or two on the job.

"Mr. Smetters, I think that Randy should return to school tomorrow, that his suspension should be lifted."

"You do, Shirleen?"

"Yes, sir." She explained about Randy's fear of falling behind, her plan to work with the family, the other boy's setting Randy up.

"Yes," the principal responded, "I know that's what he says."

"He's really sorry for what happened," Shirleen went on, "and of course we don't want his education to suffer."

Mr. Smetters leaned back in his chair and swiveled slowly to one side.

"So, the boy likes school, eh? Perhaps, then, the best guidance for him is to keep his suspension in effect."

Shirleen couldn't speak for a moment.

"I don't understand, sir. What do you mean?"

He swiveled back, fixed her with his eyes.

"You say the boy is sorry and wants to return to school, that you and the parents will be working with him. Fine. But the question in *my* mind is this: Has he learned?"

Shirleen was silent.

"When I say 'learned,' I'm not talking about anything we can teach him in a classroom–arithmetic and such. I'm talking about something more important, *far* more important. I'm talking about moral values."

He went on then about moral correction in the young, how small infractions eventually grew into violent and despicable acts. Morally inferior children grew into morally inferior adults with no sense of responsibility. Their beloved community would deteriorate. When he stopped talking, Shirleen tried to think as she made one last entreaty.

"Sir, is there some other way he could be punished? You see, I feel responsibility toward *both* his personal development–the morals and all–and his education. I wonder if we can't help the one without hurting the other."

The principal hesitated, his expression blank, then again swiveled away.

"Maybe. I'll let you know."

She learned of his decision the following morning as she sat in her office at the high school. The phone rang and one of Randy's teachers, sounding upset, asked her to come to the grade school right away.

"Why? What's the matter?"

"The principal is having a public slapping! Of Randy!"

"What?"

"He's assembling the entire school. Then he's going to stand up on the stage and slap Randy's face. His parents agreed to it. It's the only way he can get back in school."

"You must be joking. Aren't you?"

"No, Shirleen, I'm not. And Mr. Smetters says he's doing it on *your* advice!"

Feeling suddenly dizzy, Shirleen hung up and rested her head in her arms. As the dizziness passed, a familiar anger swirled up from somewhere below her heart, gathering at her temples and heating her.

The auditorium was full by the time she arrived. There were a good many adults as well as the children. Randy sat in a chair on the stage, sidelong to the audience, and his parents were seated behind him, sharing in his guilt. Mr. Smetters stood before the boy, removing Randy's glasses, handing them to a teacher who stepped back to give the principal room.

Whap!

Randy's face was twisted toward the audience and Mr. Smetters was reaching back to deliver a second blow.

"Stop it, you bastard!"

Shirleen ran up to the stage and stood below the principal.

"You son of a bitch! Slapping little boys! Go to hell with your stupid, self-righteous morality! All he wants is to get back in school, but you have to make a *spectacle* of him, show off your sick, perverted *authority*! Your need for power, to compensate for everything you lack as a *person*!"

Mr. Smetters leaned away from her, shaken. Everyone else in the place was frozen and silent. Randy watched her through his tears, but he too was unmoving.

"You talk so much about morality," Shirleen continued, "then you do something like this! You're just covering up your urge for power—wanting to see people suffer while *you* control them! You *bastard*!"

The principal's arms hung limply at his sides. He looked out confusedly over the audience. Shirleen turned and met a multitude of shocked expressions, a sea of bewilderment and fear. They didn't understand. Why was she shouting obscenities in their school? Maybe she was crazy. A counselor but crazy herself.

The nearest exit was on one side of the stage. Shirleen ran for it and no one made an effort to stop her.

———•———

We were in the conference room at our facility, Luverna and myself facing Dr. Greenberg across the table. He was engrossed in the new report I'd brought. A plate of brownies, brought in by Mrs. Arnold, sat conspicuously before us. Dr. Greenberg had enthusiastically tried one but then neglected it as my report absorbed his interest. He was middle-aged, heavy for a doctor, and wore thick glasses below his curly hair.

"Well," he intoned as the report dropped from his hands. His expression was one of enlightenment, but solemn. He hesitated, making a steeple of his hands, then continued.

"Lot of pain in this woman, deep down, been there forever. Almost." He gave me a friendly look. "Great job by the way, eliciting so much from her."

I gave a slight shrug.

"But the pain," he went on, "always there, the fear of more. The fear. Well. I'll have to see her, no question. Not today but block off next time–the whole period. Or, if you can swing a special appointment–"

Luverna gave a disconsolate look.

"Good one, doctor. The budget? Block off a session, yes, as long as Mrs. Arnold–"

"I'll talk to her myself. This is important, vital. The duration of suffering here, the long-standing lack of therapy, should give it the highest priority."

"It's strange how she fell through the cracks," said Luverna. "You'd think that somewhere along the line, with all the contacts she must have had, someone would have gotten her effective treatment. That professionals would have picked up on it, helped her."

Greenberg removed his glasses, studied them as he responded.

"It speaks to the sad state of public services. Those most in need can drift for years, decades, floating on the fringe of society. Testimony to the low ebb of humanitarianism."

He put his glasses back on and squinted at me.

"It's amazing how she opened up to you, after we'd had so little success. *No* success. There must have been some key, something that unlocked her to you."

"Tom's modest about his success," said Luverna.

"I don't mean a technique or skill necessarily–no offense, Tom–but a circumstance of some sort, a chance factor, a quirk. As if you remind her of someone or something exempt from her resistance, so she can open the album of her past to you."

"It's not always very clear," I said, "and there are many periods totally blank. Not to mention her entire later life."

"Those decades of apparent wandering," said Luverna.

Greenberg appeared thoughtful.

"Perhaps that time can be investigated. I have my contacts in the courts. We'd want to establish the veracity of her accounts, anyway."

I listened carefully, trying to picture what might be down the road. What material had I provided, I wondered, that might lead to Shirleen's identification?

"Well," said Luverna, "it seems we're making real progress. I feel optimistic. And proud of you, Tom. It's your work that finally put things on track for Shirleen."

"No question about it," Greenberg added, reaching for his unfinished brownie.

I smiled modestly.

"And in case I forget," he said looking at Luverna, "please let her know that I found these delicious!"

Wry smiles were exchanged as the psychiatrist nibbled.

Case Entry: Doe, Shirleen

Client described at length her long drive northward to see Jim. She took expressways at first, but then she was on smaller roads, gliding past dormant forests and struggling farms abandoned to winter. Occasionally there were snowflakes in the air, and she'd think of the holiday seasons she'd known and the nicer ones that she'd imagined. And yet continually she'd found herself in sullen, oppressive places, alone and uninspired. Nobody seemed to care anymore about the delicate, the beautiful, the true and fair.

There was someone, though, who would never put her down, who'd given her the spark of life and would renew her now when she needed him again. He'd been confused when she called, but he must have been happy too and he said all right come. There was another who might be there but somehow they'd get some time together and he'd speak to her in the soft, strong tones of many seasons ago.

As she neared the city, industrial sheds and metallic junk gradually replaced the gray farms and blackened forests. She wasn't sure how to find the address, so she stopped at a gas station for new directions. The man was friendly and told her to enjoy her stay in the city. It made her feel good, more confident that she was doing the right thing. The happiest time of her life had been those few months with Jim, and she hadn't even realized it. She hadn't seen the absurdity of trying to improve on perfection.

It was growing dark by the time she found his building. The snowflakes were blowing in gusts over the pavement, where leaves and paper were scattered also. She locked her car and struggled against the wind up to Jim's building. The inner door was unlocked and the stairs very quiet, as if waiting for her to tread them. She knew which door was his and the thought of running away presented itself again on the dark, smooth surface before her. When it faded for a moment, she knocked quickly before it could return.

"Oh. You made it."

"Hi, Jim."

"Come on in."

He'd put on weight, especially around his stomach, and his hair was cut short. It was darker than she remembered it, and his eyes were lighter, or maybe shallower.

"What are you doing these days?" he asked.

"Well, I had a job in community mental health, but I just left it."

There was a woman coming in from the kitchen.

"This is my wife, Marie."

His *wife*? She had dark hair, long and wavy, but seemed a little overweight. She was wearing an apron and had her hands in the pockets. She smiled but it was a courtesy smile, like the light inside a car.

"Would you like a beer?"

"Uh, no. Thanks"

"How about you, Jim?"

"Sure, I'll have one."

"Coffee, Shirleen?"

"No, nothing. Nothing for me."

Marie left the room, clearly at ease and maybe amused, Shirleen thought. She acted as if she owned the place. But then, here was Jim now married to her. Shirleen wondered what had happened to the philosophy, the poetry of his life.

"Are you still an activist?" she blurted.

He was startled, then something like embarrassed.

"Uh, I go bowling sometimes. But aside from that, I'm either at work or with Marie."

There was a moment of silence. Jim laughed slightly to break it and, for a fleeting instant, Shirleen saw the man she'd known in the monk's cell.

"It's been a long time," he said. "We're different people now."

There was a sound then that she couldn't believe she was hearing, on this night and at this place. Marie was striding quickly into the room as the noise continued. She set down two cans of beer and then quickly retreated.

"You'll have to excuse me. Eric's awake."

Jim was smiling as he watched Marie go. Shirleen looked down, waiting for his fascination to pass. The air felt like gelatin around her.

"How old is he?"

"Going on three months."

It was gone: everything he had been and hoped to be. He was a different man now. The past was irretrievable.

"I'm starting computer school in January. Nights, of course. We'll be moving when Eric gets older and I'll need a better job."

"What are you doing now, Jim? What *are you*, I mean."

"Still driving the forklift. Thought I could hook on as a mechanic, but it didn't work out. Somebody's friend got the job."

"They're talking about amnesty back home."

"I know."

"Do you think you'd go back?"

He hesitated, looking down in thought.

"There's a lot of things to consider."

Marie brought out the baby and gave him to Shirleen to hold. Staying for dinner was suggested, and watching something on TV, but Shirleen felt a desperate need to leave. Jim offered to walk her to her car, but Shirleen said no. She wanted only to escape. The wind had eased outside and a thin layer of snow had covered the neighborhood. She ignored her tears as she brushed the snow off her car, then off her coat. She didn't look back at the window of their apartment, even as she pulled away, fiddling with the heater instead. She'd seen Jim for the final time when she'd turned from him to descend the stairs.

Until quite recently.

———•◦•———

It was the middle of the night. We were in Luverna's bed, she breathing steadily in sleep. Minimal light came through from outside, allowing me to sense forms as I lay awake, reflecting on our expired evening.

We'd had dinner at a Chinese buffet, making the trips back and forth and amusing each other with our selections. It was in a mall, so later we browsed past indoor store windows, avoiding the raw wind outside. Luverna stopped before a display of engagement sets, but we moved on with vague smiles. She showed more spirit before a luggage display.

"Why don't we take a vacation, Tom?"

"Where would you like to go?"

"I don't know, some place warm."

"Warm would be nice."

"Though you're good with cold, too. Maybe you like it better."

"I could always handle it pretty well."

We went on to a store with funny clothing, then to a bookstore we decided to enter, our banter growing slightly more serious. Later, in the car, Luverna relaxed with her head back, eyes closed, while I drove to her apartment. We were becoming close, I saw, in more subtle ways now. Quiet understandings were developing.

Now, in her bed, I sensed the empty wine glasses out in the living room, the CD still in the machine though the music had run its course. It was the afterglow of intimacy, a time for sleeping though only one of us was doing so.

I was actually more awake than I'd been all night. I was thinking of my last report on Shirleen, mailed so it would reach Luverna the coming workday. I wouldn't be at the facility when she read it. I didn't plan on going there ever again. My last talk with Shirleen had exhausted my capacity to illuminate her past. It was up to Greenberg now to fill in the gaps, to assign meanings and suggest a plan. For me the road ahead was a mystery, as it always had been since Marie became distant, remaining herself while I, Jim/Tom, reverted painfully to my college persona.

"Don't you realize those times are over?" she'd demanded. "Gone forever!"

"I'm not *trying* to slide back," I'd said. "It just comes to me by itself."

I had to walk around, quietly slipped out of the covers. Luverna wouldn't be surprised, I knew, if she woke and found me gone. I hadn't always stayed the night, what with Mrs. Arnold's scrutiny. And Luverna was well accustomed to being alone in bed.

Eric was a man himself now, solid, working in business under better mentors than me. Marie had remarried after the divorce, her spouse a serious contractor.

I passed the coffee table where I knew the wine glasses stood, taking care to not upset them. I thought of the CD still in the machine, recalling the music we'd enjoyed, but left the disk where it was to avoid making noise. I dressed in the dark. Shirleen's visit may have started things, I thought, brought me eventually to this room, this secret exit from a lover, a job, and a former lover. But maybe it would've happened anyway, memories and sentiment driving me to ramble until I found her, set things right in some way, helped her if only a little. I couldn't undo what had happened to her, couldn't have prevented it in the first place. But maybe I'd changed her direction, her downward spiral, so that others more competent than me could help her salvage something from life.

I found my coat, looked around in the dark, said goodbye in my mind to Luverna. I slipped out the door as quietly as I could. I pulled away in my car.

I'd ramble on, I knew, my own issues as unresolved as ever. My efforts with Shirleen, I realized, had been for my own benefit as much as hers: to lend value to my existence, some affirmation. But the forces around me and those deep within were, as always, too great for my actions to make a difference. I had never been truly romantic, yet never a good realist. I wasn't quite a schizoid, but was basically unreachable, in my own personal limbo. And the worst part of it–or maybe the best–was this: I liked it.

I drove on into the night.